EVERYTHING LOVELY, EFFORTLESS, SAFE

EVERYTHING LOVELY, EFFORTLESS, SAFE

a novel

JENNY HOLLOWELL

A Holt Paperback

Henry Holt and Company   New York

Holt Paperbacks
Henry Holt and Company, LLC
Publishers since 1866
175 Fifth Avenue
New York, New York 10010
www.henryholt.com

A Holt Paperback® and ⓟ® are registered trademarks of
Henry Holt and Company, LLC.

Distributed in Canada by H. B. Fenn and Company Ltd.

Library of Congress Cataloging-in-Publication Data

Hollowell, Jenny.
  Everything lovely, effortless, safe : a novel / Jenny Hollowell.
    p. cm.
  "A Holt Paperback."
  ISBN 978-0-8050-9119-9
  1. Young women—Fiction.   2. Actresses—Fiction.   3. Hollywood
(Los Angeles, Calif.)—Fiction.   I. Title.
  PS3608.O49425E94 2010
  813'.6—dc22   2009022721

Henry Holt books are available for special promotions and
premiums. For details contact: Director, Special Markets.

First Holt Paperbacks Edition 2010

Designed by Kelly S. Too

Printed in the United States of America

1 3 5 7 9 10 8 6 4 2

For Daron and Lowe

It's all make-believe, isn't it?
—Marilyn Monroe

EVERYTHING LOVELY, EFFORTLESS, SAFE

prologue

Ask Birdie how she got here and she'll pretend she doesn't remember. "Honestly," she'll say, "it all blends together." She doesn't want to talk about the past. It's only cocktail talk but still everyone wants a story. That's Los Angeles for you. Everything's a pitch. Sell the beginning and give the end a twist.

The truth is rarely filmic. Lies are better. Once she told a director she was sleeping with, or who, more accurately, was sleeping with her: *My whole family is dead. We were in a car accident together. My mother, father, and sister were killed and I am the only survivor.* What did he say? "What an amazing story," which meant that he was sorry but also that it would make a great movie.

Semantics, anyway. There was never any car accident but still she has lost them all.

Ask Birdie how she got here and she will smile and laugh and look down into her glass. Two things she's good at: drinking and keeping secrets. In the melting ice cubes she sees the past.

1

At her agent's insistence her bio contains the basics: 1979, Powhatan, Virginia. Even that doesn't matter. Redmond changed it to 1983. "Whoever said thirty is the new twenty-two wasn't trying to get you work." Proof positive: no one really wants the truth.

What she omits besides her real age: her early filmography (though there were no cameras rolling) where she built her acting résumé.

The Hallelujah Days, 1979–1986. The south side, the dusty book-shelves full of Bibles, the dim rooms, the pleases and thank-yous, the do-as-I-says and just-you-waits. The chained dogs barking in the neighbor's yard. Mother lying for too long in her bedroom, day after day, in the dark.

Also: hand-me-downs, a cat named Sofia, a basement full of crickets, a bedroom with purple wallpaper. Her father coming and going on missionary trips to Places Where the Need Is Greater. Birdie's first Bible (it had a green cover and she drew hearts and flowers in the margins). Church five days a week and, on the other two, preaching in the park until it got dark. "Do you know the Truth?" she asks people as they pass. She offers the Truth in the form of a pamphlet with a full-color picture of Paradise printed on its cover.

(This is where Birdie feels compelled to tell the nonexistent interviewer: no, we weren't white trash, no, I wasn't beaten. You're screening the wrong movie. In this one, I watched the sky for signs that the End was coming and was therefore afraid of thunderstorms.)

More about her mother. When she slept, she wore a velvet sleep mask with a pair of open eyes painted on it. This reminded Birdie of God, of how He can see you when He is sleeping, if He even sleeps.

The Birth of Desire, July 25, 1987. Birdie awaits the birth of her sister at her Worldly (Presbyterian, which is the same as not believing anything, according to their pastor) grand-mother's house while Mother and Father are at the hospital.

Her aunts (it is hard to believe those creatures were her mother's sisters) recline around the pool like goddesses, lis-tening to a boom box, rubbing oil into their skin, smoking cigarettes, and sipping Tab. They dive into the pool and swim down to touch the bottom, their gold jewelry flashing like fish in the deep blue water. They give Birdie ice cream and take her photograph. They braid her hair and let her wear their sunglasses.

A magnolia tree leans high above them, dropping seedpods into the swimming pool as the breeze shifts. The pods float for a moment and then sink through the water, pulled toward the black drain at the bottom of the pool. No one knows yet that Birdie's sister will not be born alive. If they knew what grief awaited her, the aunts would not talk about Birdie's mother as they do. *Bitten by the spirit,* one of them says, rub-bing oil into her legs. *Have you seen their house?* another mur-murs. *Bitten by fleas is more like it.* The aunts laugh. Birdie listens, treading water. Her body is cold but her face burns hot with rushing blood. She is thinking that whatever her mother is she must also be. *We have a cat,* she says suddenly and the aunts fall silent. Seedpods keep falling one by one into the water. *That's where the fleas come from,* she says. The aunts nod and look at each other and stub out their cigarettes. *How did you get so smart?* they say, pulling her out of the pool.

Their tan boyfriends arrive, wearing polo shirts, smiling broadly, smelling (she knows now) like Tanqueray. Chip, Tad, Henry. They flirt with her. *You're only seven?* Tad says. *You look ten.* The boyfriends fish pennies from their pockets and distribute them. *Remember,* they say. *Don't tell your wish to anyone.* Then they pitch the coins into the courtyard fountain.

After the aunts have left on their dates, after her grandmother is home, after dinner in the kitchen with the cook, after her bath, after everyone has gone to bed, Birdie wanders the endless hallways of the unfamiliar house. The still, deep swimming pool, the courtyard full of statues, the bubbling fountain, the heavy crystal ashtrays. The solarium full of gently nodding orchids. The wallpaper in the foyer, painted with scenes of rural life in China—men in pointed straw hats resting under a pagoda, leading a mule cart, fetching water. Room after room heavy with stillness, doors slightly ajar, shoes scattered on the carpets, dresses sprawled on empty beds, the air glinting with particles of face powder.

At the bottom of the courtyard fountain, she spies the coins they threw in to make wishes, even though she knows wishes are prayers to Satan for things too selfish to ask of God. Her penny flashes on the floor of the fountain as hard and shining and wicked as the wish that accompanied it. She remembers, with shame: *to be someone else.*

Saving Things, 1987–1996. The house seems so empty, Mother says. And so she fills it slowly, with empty boxes and old newspapers and broken things. Everything is saved, just in case.

The rooms grow smaller, lined with what might be needed later—broom handles and catalogs and phone books and coat hangers—until there is no room for anyone, not even ghosts. *This is all just trash*, Birdie says, but Mother shakes her head. Dad sighs and rubs her shoulder. In this darkness he blends right into the wallpaper.

As the rooms grow smaller Birdie grows bigger. Soon it will be easy to believe that she is only a visitor.

Someone Else, 1993. Birdie stands in her bedroom, studying a picture she has torn from a fashion magazine: a girl with her hair in her eyes sprawled across an enormous bed, wearing peach satin underwear trimmed with bits of yellow tulle. A matching corset lies in shadow, discarded on the floor below her. A mirror on the wall above the bed reflects the girl's bare, luminous torso.

Birdie locks the door, consults the photograph again, and stands at her full-length mirror. She pushes her hair forward. Her hair isn't quite long enough but she gets the desired effect. She squints until she looks hungry and dissatisfied. She takes off her shirt, but the bra won't do; it is plain and white, like her. She removes it. She once read somewhere that breasts should look like pastries, good enough to eat. Hers are smallish cupcakes, but still she can see their appeal. They look untouched: soft white peaks.

She flips off the overhead light and focuses her gooseneck desk lamp on the floor in front of her mirror. Then she lies back across the floor, the pile of the rose-colored carpet soft against her back and the warmth of the lamplight on her eyelids and breasts. She looks over into the mirror. *You have a secret*, she tells herself, adjusting her expression until hanging there suddenly, with her hair in her eyes and the light washing away her features, is someone else, as lovely and remote as the girl in the photograph. The light from the desk lamp carves a line below her cheekbones and hangs shadows like moons beneath her breasts. Her pupils contract, turning small and bright and black. The light becomes a flashbulb, a spotlight, a light with a million eyes hidden behind it. The eyes watch her, waiting for her to do something.

Hi there, she whispers.

One Small Step, October 1996. They meet in a movie theater. She is alone and he spots her from across the auditorium. Then he moves, seat by seat, until he is right next to her. She pretends not to notice until he whispers into her ear, *Wanna go somewhere? Yes*, she says.

He drives her to the Blue Light. His name is Wes. He is twenty-one years old and from the other side of the river. He buys her a drink and she feels it immediately. She asks for another. It is like wading into a lake, its murky depths turning her slowly weightless. Soon enough, she is floating.

They leave the bar, stumbling out into the parking lot, and then walk for a little while until they reach an empty playground. There, they spin around on the whirligig and climb the monkey bars. They sit side by side on the swings, twisting them slowly so that the chains wind tight above them, pulling them up into the air. Then they let go and the chains unwind, spinning down like corkscrews and then flinging them to the ground. Wes kisses her there, his hands exploring her hair, her dress, her breasts. He is looking for the answer to the question he asks next: *Want to come with me?* She searches her brain for words but there is only one left.

A little while later they are at his apartment. A mirror hangs on his bedroom wall. She turns away from it. (The mirror has become like God, gazing back at her, always assessing. In certain lights, forgiving.)

He pulls her clothes away, dropping them like stepping-stones across the carpet. She lies back on the bedspread. It is like being packed into a suitcase or being sucked through a straw. It is like being smaller than any small thing, so small that she turns inside out and grows back again. So that she is herself, only reversed, like in the mirror. The same size, only flatter, smoother, calmer.

Let me take your picture, he says, *lie back*, and she does, across the rumpled bed. It is easy to say yes. She is only surface, the prospect of her own beauty flattening her thoughts and burying them deep beneath her, where they whisper back and forth in the dark. Whatever will come later, the die has been cast. The night is happening and she cannot take it back.

The camera loves you, he whispers, and she believes him. Other eyes are more reliable than her own, prone as hers are to seeking out imperfection. She hopes that God is like Wes—like the men who will come later—full of appreciation for her overall effect and less concerned with specifics.

She lies in that dim light for a while. She is skimming the surface of something, skipping like a pebble over still water. Enough velocity and she could go on like this forever. (But also, the movie camera would imply, with a slow turning away to the ceiling, then down past their bodies, the coverlet, the carpet, all accompanied by the sound of the ticking clock and the clicking shutter: she could sink like a stone.)

A Sin of Omission, 1997. She is preaching in the park with her mother when suddenly Wes is standing in front of her. Mother thrusts a pamphlet into his hand. Wes glances at Birdie, not recognizing her at first. Then there is the moment when his eyes slowly narrow, like a gear is turning inside him. He stares, comparing, she knows, this girl with the other one. She didn't tell him about this life, but doesn't everyone have two? There is the life you live for your parents and then the life for you.

He turns and walks away from them, glancing backward just once and then striding on, faster. It is not unusual for people to avoid them, passing quickly. What is unusual is Birdie falling to her knees, with her face in her hands.

There, there, Mother says, crouching over her, as distant from Birdie in that moment as she will ever be. Then she whispers the truest words she will ever speak: *Not everyone wants the Truth*.

Waiting, 1997–1998. She saw Wes again only that time in the park. She never sees the photographs though for a while she waits for them. As she waits she cuts back vines from her windowpane, she drops coins into a mason jar, she smuggles newspapers from the hallway to the trash, clearing a path. As she waits, she screams at a camel cricket leaping over her foot, she screams from a dream of the Resurrection, bones moving in a grave, she screams on a sled that races down a snowy hillside. *You frighten so easily*, her parents say, her body jumping when the doorbell would ring. *Yes*, she says. Her head is full of secrets shifting like sand. She is waiting for the photographs to be delivered and opened and scattered across the kitchen table—her sins excavated, her tedious little life dismantled—maybe she even wishes for it, but they never arrive.

The Young Elder, 1998. Father has just returned from a missionary trip to southwest Virginia and has brought back with him a young elder named Judah Common. Her parents invite him to dinner.

Brother Common eats two helpings of everything and

does not seem to have any judgments about the contents of the house. *I see you recycle* is all he says, smiling. He plays his guitar after dinner, several hymns as well as "Come On Baby Light My Fire," but he changes the words to "Come On Baby Change My Tire" to keep the content moral. Birdie can't help but think that either way the song is asking her to make his life easier.

Later her parents go into the kitchen to clean up from dinner leaving Birdie and Brother Common alone in the living room, with the door cracked, to talk.

What are your plans? he asks.

I don't know, she says. *It all seems pretty complicated.*

Even as she says the words, she realizes how stupid she sounds, how unprepared. She has spent her life so far waiting for an End, a judgment that would determine her worthiness for whatever followed, but the End just wouldn't arrive. She does not know what God thinks of her or what she thinks of herself, only that everything—life and death, goals and plans—seemed hopelessly theoretical, bound as it all was to the assumption that He could show up at any time and put an End to all of it.

Sometimes, says Brother Common, putting his hand on hers (a nice enough hand, a hand that is warm but not clammy, that is soft but still strong), *it's not as complicated as you think. Sometimes an answer is provided.*

An Answer Is Provided, 1999. They marry the following summer in the church. Birdie is relieved when on their wedding night Judah does not guess that there was ever another.

This time is different. A sunlit afternoon dissolves into a stormy evening and Judah heaves above her, as serious and gray-faced as the weather. Afterward he keeps sighing heavily as though he has run a long distance. He speaks abstractly about being yoked together. (A camera would study her eyes, defocused as she stares at the window, water sliding down the pane as Judah murmurs, as thunder rumbles. She is thinking of two oxen pulling a cart, persisting uphill through cold sheets of gray rain.)

What Was Expected, 2000. In the grocery store Birdie runs into Mr. Ogden, the drama teacher from her old high school. She had only taken his class for the one required semester but when she would read a monologue he would lean against the edge of his desk, dragging his index finger across his lip as he watched her. He would nod almost imperceptibly as she spoke, as though she were convincing him of something he hadn't previously considered. *You have talent*, he told her, and though she suspected he told everybody that, she had wanted to believe him.

Mr. Ogden smiles and approaches. *What are you still doing here?* he says. *I figured the next time I saw you it would be in a movie.*

Really? she says.

Yes, he says. *We all want to be immortalized, but you . . . you have the face for it. You should be in Hollywood by now, doing us proud.*

Oh, Mr. Ogden, she says. *Soon enough.*

He smiles. *Yes, soon enough*, he says. He surveys her body appreciatively. *There is always a way for the young and lovely.*

When she catches her reflection in the freezer doors, she must acknowledge that she had expected more of herself. She hovers like a ghost in the glass door, the rows of frozen vegetables inside more substantial than her own image. What was she doing spending her (young, lovely) life cooking dinner for a (hopelessly good, hopelessly serious) man who rarely laughs, who calls her Sister Common when they're at church, who undresses in the dark?

Place Your Bets, 2000. That night Judah sleeps beside her, no pain apparent in him, no unspoken fears or unanswered questions. His body rises and falls as he breathes. He is full of dinner and holy spirit. Yes, he is full and so he sleeps.

Birdie lies beside him, troubled by his peace. Dissatisfaction is what God wants of everyone, is it not, to find enough wrong with this world and one's stake in it to wager this life on the next one? The next life will be better, or at least that's the rumor, the life where everything comes together just as you hoped. And so, greedy for Paradise, you gamble your life. That's all this is: a wager. You agree to call it God's Will if you win and God's Plan if you lose.

Judah stirs. He opens his eyes enough to see that Birdie is still awake. *What is it?* he whispers, reaching for her. He is good. He is a good and faithful man who smells like the aftershave he wears only because she gave it to him.

Nothing, she says, in his arms. (In a movie of this moment, the camera would not move. No, the lens would remain on her face, waiting for her expression to betray something. Then she stirs. Her eyelids flutter as she closes her eyes, not to sleep but to dream.)

The Savings Add Up, 2001. She does not take the car or anything of value except her clothes (and only as many as will fit into one suitcase). She does take some money but only money that adheres to a specific formula. Whatever money she has saved by clipping coupons (she calculates a total of approximately $10 a week, when you include the double coupon amount she gets by shopping on Tuesdays) she takes with her. Eighty-seven weeks of marriage at ten dollars a week is $870.

That way she is only taking what she has earned, in a way, and when she leaves the slate will be clean. She will not owe anyone anything.

Going West and the Rest, 2001. In Powhatan, she leaves a letter that says:

> To Judah and My Parents,
>
> I don't know if you will be surprised to find this note. I am not surprised to be writing it, though I know it will hurt you and I hate to do that. But you have to know I have no other choice. I have been a liar and a hypocrite. I have tried to be a Believer, but I am not. Every day, I am full of doubt. I would rather be honest about my feelings in this life than lie to preserve an eternal hope I am unsure of. Let's hope God understands my decision. I'm sorry.
>
> Love, Birdie.
>
> PS—Don't try to find me. I'm safe, but I'm going somewhere far away.

The bus ride to Los Angeles takes two days, seventeen hours, and five minutes. For the first day, she imagines that Judah is following her, that when the bus stops at a rest area he will be standing there stormy-faced, waiting to take her back. But by the morning of the second day, as serpentine mountain roads begin to flatten and give way to low flat stretches of highway, her escape begins to feel real. Nothing is familiar—the scenery, her fellow passengers, the gravity and speed of the bus as it rockets westward past little towns, sprawling lights, empty desert, road signs. Her face reflected back at her in the thick safety glass of the bus window appears ghostly and doubled. She glances back and forth between both sets of eyes and watches the reflections react—her fractured face bobs and shifts across the glass.

2

Nine years she has been here. Her résumé gets longer, but no more distinguished:

- Woman in the Crowd, 2001. *The Long River.*
- Girl Who Screams, 2002. *The Ball of Terror.*
- Pretty Girl, 2003. *By the Sea.*
- Overdrawn Customer, 2003. Bank of California commercial.
- Bikini Girl, 2004. Hops Beer commercial.
- Amber's Roommate, 2005. *All That Burns: The Amber Tiffany Story.*

Her speaking roles have usually been in commercials: "What do you mean I'm overdrawn?" and "I wish the scent of my fabric softener lasted longer." She has done a few plays, though she doesn't like the stage; the proximity to the audience disconcerts her. Their judgment is so tangible, so near that she can hear it in their sighs and rustles and coughs. If hundreds of pairs of eyes are going to be watching her perform, she does not want to be in the room. That is the beauty of the movies: on any given night, scores of people can watch the fifty-foot Movie You while the Actual You is home safely in bed.

Much of Birdie's recent work has been as a lighting double. She stands in one spot while the crew adjusts the lights, while the camera assistant measures the distance from the camera lens to her cheek. When everything is perfect, she makes way for the leading lady. Sometimes she doubles on-camera as well, at a long distance, or as their hands, or as their naked body in the shower or sliding into bed. Either way, the job is the same—hours spent as someone else's body, faceless and blurry—no expression, no release.

Doing this work she has met a lot of famous actors, famous directors too, and they invite her to their parties and more than once a movie star has wrapped her arm around Birdie's shoulders and said, "Hey everyone. This is me! Have you met me?"

Like tonight. Birdie is at the home of Melena Duvall, star of *The Evening Dawn* and hostess for a continuation of its wrap party. Her house is improbably cantilevered on the shoulders of the Hollywood Hills, a stone's throw from Griffith Park. Birdie sits with Redmond nursing a drink on the veranda—a seemingly endless expanse of swimming pool and slate and glass that finally drops off into thin air. The city lies supplicant beneath the party, its lights sparkling and winking as if it existed solely for the partygoers' enchant-ment, just another lovely accessory that would be packed up along with the rented glassware and returned at the end of the night.

Sour-faced girls covered with gold dust and wearing biki-nis made of interlocking metal plates stalk party guests with platters full of tiny food: tiny vegetable dumplings, tiny sea-weed cones heaped with raw tuna, tiny medallions of pork, each adorned with a sprig of rosemary. The platters never diminish. Partygoers dance to hip-hop on the veranda or lounge on giant silk pillows around the stone fireplace, mur-muring, staring at the flames. The house itself appears to be lit by a thousand pinpoint sources, like the inside of a honey-comb, amber and refracted. Strangers kiss deeply along the candlelit corridors.

Melena has lost her shoes and darts around the party

barefoot, shouting to no one in particular, "Do you love this song? Oh my god, I love this song!" before finally jumping, fully clothed, into the swimming pool. Legions follow.

Birdie whispers to Redmond, "Cokeheads sure like to swim."

He gives a low chuckle. "No, they just like to jump into swimming pools. Love that splash! Give her some credit—look, she didn't even spill her drink."

"Redmond, that's pool water. Let's hope she takes a sip. God, did you hear how she introduced me? 'Guys, this is my ass! Don't I have an amazing ass?' Like I didn't *also* have a head. I'm . . . an ass. Literally. I'm so sick of these narcissists."

"Easy, tiger. The veranda has ears. Want me to list all of the narcissists we can't afford to alienate?"

"I'm serious, Redmond. I don't want to do this work anymore. This . . . appendage work. I'm a glorified crash test dummy."

"You're being dramatic. It pays the bills. Not to mention your dues."

"I'm done with dues, Redmond. I've had nine years of them. It's a legitimacy issue. Who is going to take me seriously? I go into an audition and they ask what I've been in. Saying I was Melena Duvall's ass in *The Evening Dawn* isn't winning me any points."

"Makes you memorable."

"So is a bearded lady." Birdie drains her glass and rises from the table. "I'm getting another."

At this moment Melena staggers from the pool emitting a high-pitched squeal. "Birdie! You're not going!"

"No. Just getting another drink."

"Ohmygod let somebody else do that." Melena stabs her finger through the air toward one of the gold-dust-covered girls. "You. Can you get my friend a drink?"

"That's not necessary," says Birdie.

"That's what she's here for!" Melena insists.

"Of course," says the girl. "What are you drinking?"

"Scotch," says Birdie, smiling apologetically. The girl nods and stalks away.

"Scotch!" says Melena. "You're such a badass. You're like, Hi. I drink scotch. No big deal." She throws an arm around Birdie's shoulders, dripping pool water down her back. "Wait, don't move. We need a picture. Redmond, if I get my camera will you take one?"

"Absolutely," says Redmond. "Love to."

"Good. I'll get a camera." Melena turns and skips toward the house, calling back over her shoulder, "Seriously, Birdie, don't move!"

Birdie turns toward Redmond. He is holding his hand in front of his mouth, suppressing a laugh. "Don't move!" he mimics. "Seriously!"

"You see this?" Birdie points emphatically at her feet. "I *never* move. This is what I *do* now, Redmond. I stand still. Professionally."

"Come on," he says. "These things progress organically."

"Organically?" she says. "Are we farming? Do me a favor. Make it fast and artificial."

"I am just saying, again, that there is no such thing as an overnight success. How many times do I need to say that?"

"A million, Redmond. One million times. Keep telling me."

"Forget it," he says, placing his drink on the ground beside him.

"Don't be mad. I can't help it. I'm drunk, I think." She looks around the patio. "Speaking of . . . where's that scotch?"

"I'm sure that gold slave is spitting in it as we speak," Redmond says, lowering his voice to a stage whisper. "Listen. Melena Duvall is the prototype! She's been around for, what, twelve years?"

"And then she got *Mind Games. Mind Games* did it. I. Need. A. *Mind. Games.*" She pokes her index finger into his chest with each word.

"You'll get your *Mind Games*," Redmond says, grabbing her finger. "Soon."

Birdie is silent. She is tired of soon. *Soon* is round and smooth, without *never*'s honest jagged edges. Soon is like the End of the World, always approaching but never arriving. Soon is the excuse people use when nothing ever happens on time.

"Listen," Redmond continues. "Melena was modeling bathing suits and jumping the wrong bones as recently as last year. I'm talking . . . Game. Show. Hosts." He draws the lapels of his jacket up around his neck and pretends to shiver.

"Ah, yes, well, she's known for being . . . cooperative," Birdie says, staring past Redmond, letting the end of her sentence become silence. She lets the party wash over her—the quivering candlelight, the smooth stone walkways, the deep blue water, the golden limbs, the music so loud it seems to originate inside her, the utter beauty of everything, beauty that can hardly be called beauty because it is so ubiquitous, so liquid, so senseless.

Redmond follows her gaze. "Yes, cooperative," he says finally. "And what, pray tell, can that get you? Besides, of course, obligatory heaps of existential angst? Twelve large a picture, four thousand square feet in the Hills, and an infinity pool to cry into. Sweet little Birdie. Do you know how long you can cry into an infinity pool?" Redmond widens his eyes and takes Birdie's face in his hands. "Forever."

3

This is the routine. Birdie wakes at seven and is in her car by seven-thirty, easing past the low Venice bungalows, the quiet creeping green of cultivated plants, the still canals, the hum of distant mowers, the careful stone pathways, the faded pink apartments, the punctuation of the sun peeping from behind a line of palms as she drives, sleepy-eyed, to buy coffee on the way to the gym. With the previous evening's indulgences still metabolizing in her body, she goes. Once she is on the treadmill, she can run for five miles before she starts to feel tired. The air-conditioning vents on the ceiling gasp along with her as she runs. The treadmills are arranged in rows and if someone is on the treadmill in front of her she focuses on their shoulders. As the sweat breaks and rolls down their back, she pictures a race—one in which she will let them think they are winning until the very end and then she will burst past them. These imagined victories sustain her in some way. Each day she tries to run just a little bit farther but as soon as the digital readout clicks past five miles her limbs thicken and slow and she stops. She tells herself that her body knows best. If it's Tuesday, Thursday, or Saturday she also lifts weights. Then it's back home for a shower.

By the time she steps out of the shower it is usually close to ten. She then spends an hour grooming: applying toner and anti-aging serum and firming complex, moisturizing her face and body, brushing and flossing her teeth, gargling, pushing back her cuticles, sloughing away the rough skin on her elbows and heels, applying fade cream to her blemishes and freckles, applying mink oil to her eyelashes, plucking her eyebrows, and blow-drying her hair. The sisterhood other women have, the commonalities—their evolving bodies, the pounds lost and gained, the babies growing in stages inside them, the synchronizations—are unknown to her. Her body is a prop that others rent and so it must be maintained. There can be no sweet tastes melting on her tongue, no pleasure in food, no rescue there. Such is the tyranny of her body. She cannot disappear, as some women do, swaddling themselves in fat, securing it to their bodies like disguises, like life vests, hiding in its folds until they are ready to be seen again. And yet disappearing is the point, to be inoffensive, to be similar, to be mutable, to carry in her body a certain kind of neutrality so that when the camera finally rolls she is exactly what is expected—barely visible and so, somehow, perfect—an image that does not exist beyond the limits of the film's frame.

She applies her makeup. Enough to look like she's wearing nothing and then the slightest bit more. She greets herself in the mirror when she is finished. "Hey there," she says. "Hey there, hi there, ho there." She grins widely into the mirror and examines her teeth for lipstick. She sticks out her tongue and wiggles it. Then she tries a red carpet smile: gentle but confident, demure but sexy. Head slightly lowered, eyes looking up.

All of that talk for so long about the Apocalypse, about immortality, stayed with her in this way: she is surprised to see, in her face, that time has passed. The skin on her cheek is always less resilient today than yesterday. Her body is apparently mortal. Just small changes now—the baby fat disappearing, her cheekbones showing their prominence, the creases between her nose and mouth becoming a little more pronounced. It is hard to let go of the most fantastic aspect of her childhood beliefs—that the End is Near. In fact, the End is not coming. Or rather, the end is not capitalized. The end will find her individually, creeping over her and tugging at her beauty until it sags and unravels. At least the Apocalypse would have saved her from that.

Something else. As she opens the medicine cabinet, or as she leans over the sink, or as she reaches for the bathroom light switch, she catches glimpses of her mother in the mirror. As a child she hadn't considered the origin of her mother's lines—the furrow of her brow, the crease of her cheek, the shadow below her eyes—but now Birdie knows. The lines are the wait recorded. They are the sum of hope and time.

When she is not working, which is too often these days, the afternoon is devoted to what Redmond calls *career development*—auditions, meetings, phone calls, lunches, the occasional seminar or acting class. The brutality of callbacks: the neutral-colored walls, the outdated magazines, the hand-lettered signs, the half-baked scripts, the handshakes, the small talk, the conspiratorial wink of the video camera's Record light, the promises, the compliments, the critiques, the goodbyes. The parking lot is always a relief after those cold rooms, to see her car waiting in the far corner shade of trees, its solid blue body more familiar than any face.

Today is a movie audition, her second callback, for the role of a hooker whose pimp conscripts her as an assassin. In order to buy her freedom, she agrees to settle a score for him. The ratio of spoken lines to full frontal nude scenes is only two to one, but she gets to die, which is promising. *Dying makes you memorable*, Redmond said.

As she drives to the appointment, she practices along

with the Accent Elimination and Development CDs Redmond got for her. What Redmond calls education, Birdie calls busywork, but still she does it. Volume One is devoted to learning how to sound completely neutral, your origins unidentifiable. Volumes Two–Eight are devoted to learning specific accents: British, German, French, Indian, Spanish, Japanese, and American (Boston, New York, Chicago, Cajun, and Southern, which is now difficult for her, an accent she buried only to have to bring it back). Birdie mastered Volume One quickly and is now working on her British accent. "Pardon me," she repeats as she crawls along the 10. "Do you have the time?" She lifts her foot off the brake to roll forward a few feet and then presses it again. Lift, roll, press. She sounds good to herself, almost like the real thing, and wonders briefly if she should suggest making the murderous hooker British. She repeats, "Pardon me, do you have the time?"

An acting coach she once had, Byron Everett, used to keep photographs of his success stories hung along the walls of his studio. He called them his Wall of Fame: Rex Peters, Seamus Brand, Tandie Snyder, Daniella Goode. Their faces were smiling, triumphant, instantly recognizable, and beside each of them was Byron caught in an enthusiastic embrace. In every photograph he wore an expression of pleasant surprise. When Birdie asked him why, he said that he was truly surprised that any of them had amounted to anything. *Honestly, they are all terrible*, he said. *Just as bad as you*.

Whenever she doubted Byron, which had been often, she would look up at the photographs and imagine herself hanging there among them. After Byron left—back to New York, back to the theater, he had had enough of starfucking and frozen foreheads and goodie bags, he said—the photographs stayed with her, Seamus Brand's in particular.

She remembers every detail: Brand lit by flashbulbs, flares of white light that washed away the details of the ballroom behind him and turned the smiling faces around him into flat, grinning moons. His mouth smiled enthusiastically but his eyes were exhausted. His jacket was unbuttoned and his cowlick was untamed, a single dark curl of hair that fell across his gleaming forehead. The gold statuette in his hand appeared heavy; he held it like a dumbbell heaved up into a bicep curl. He was weary, as a prophet is weary, from his service to the people. Birdie wonders about the statuette, whether it was cold or hollow, whether anyone had ever been injured on its regal, pointed wings. She wants to run her fingers over its smooth cast surface, to hold it in her hands and be surprised by its heaviness. She would like to be tired, not from wanting something but from having it, from holding its weight aloft for everyone to see.

She gazes past the windshield and the creeping line of cars like beetle shells glinting in the sun. In this daydream, the cameras flash and the crowd roars and pants and shouts *Birdie! Birdie! Birdie!* Her name rains down on her head like flower petals. The girl that they adore is the girl she wants to be: nothing but beauty, someone else's happy dream. How beautifully, beautifully blank she could be, her failures forgotten, blasted away by the roar of her name being shouted and those lovely bright flashes of light.

The sun flashes off the roofs of cars and off the hot shimmering highway and Birdie squints now in spite of her sunglasses. She closes her eyes for a moment to these thoughts and to the sun until she is jolted back to alertness by the sound of a car horn. The stream of traffic has proceeded without her, leaving a gap. She touches her foot to the accelerator to make up the distance and returns her focus to the voice coming from her car speakers. It is easy to imagine this voice sipping tea or dressed in tweed, walking along a foggy hillside. So civilized, other lives—this lilting British accent repeating the simplest of questions, a question that she repeats now in her own stumbling imitation: *Isn't this lovely weather?*

4

"Yeah, baby," says Birdie. "Sure I like to party."

"Bitchier," the director murmurs, chewing a bite of sandwich and then suddenly coughing. He pauses and puts a napkin to his mouth, spitting out a half-chewed bite. He hands the napkin to the young woman sitting beside him. "Fucking prosciutto," he says. The woman frowns and tosses it toward the wastebasket, missing. When Birdie asked him about the accent at the outset of the audition he had frowned. When I think *hooker* I think *American*, he said.

Now he takes a drink of water and wipes his mouth with the back of his hand. "Anyway, yeah, definitely bitchier. You're sick of the scene but you have to stick it out. You want something, you know? It's your fucking freedom! So, be a real cunt. But sexy. You know what I mean?"

"Yeah," Birdie says, nodding. "Definitely." She notices the napkin is slowly creeping open, revealing the half-chewed meat inside.

"Okay," the casting director sighs, pressing Record on the video camera. "Go again."

When Birdie first arrived in Los Angeles she found herself in a place she did not recognize. It seemed that the highway was still speeding below her as she searched for the information counter, as she sat on a bench outside the bus station, as she walked to the bathroom and stood at the sink splashing her face with cold water. Although she had often envisioned being in Los Angeles—the palm trees and the ocean and the glamorous parties and the always-beautiful weather and the mostly beautiful people—she had never pictured the part where she arrived at a dreary, inhospitable bus station filled with derelicts and strangers, the part where she figured out exactly where to go.

She found a sodden flyer on the bathroom counter advertising the Hollywood Youth Hostel and soon found herself there, at the doorway to a jumble of stucco and cinder block tucked behind a strip mall near the corner of Fountain and Gower. For sixteen dollars a night she got a bed in a mixed-gender dormitory, a locker, and access to the shared showers and bathrooms. She spent a total of six and a half weeks there and it was in those chaotic, squalid days—with the masses of hair clogging the shower drains, the murky water rising and churning around her ankles, interview after interview for the lowliest of waitressing jobs and upon finding one spending twelve hours on her feet only to return to the hostel, the mold swirling along the walls like powdery gray galaxies, the man in the bunk above her who spent each night trembling and moaning, the boards holding up his mattress threatening to crash down upon her—that Birdie found herself doing something like praying.

She would lock herself in the bathroom late at night and with the light off. She would sit on the toilet seat with her head in her hands and repeat, *This is what you want. This is what you want.* (She did not claim to know what *this* was— maybe it was the movies, maybe it was Los Angeles, maybe it was sleeping in a bed alone—only that it would save her from life with Judah in Powhatan, which was its own kind of End. The other kind of End involved four horsemen on the horizon, which seemed far more unlikely and therefore less terrifying.) In the darkness of the bathroom she would not let the tears fall or even form or let the lump in her throat grow into anything other than the words *This is what you want,* until they were no longer words but just something that her mouth was doing, a sound coming out of her until someone pounded on the door. Then she would emerge from the dark interior of the bathroom to find someone waiting, always a stranger, always frightening in some way (booze-soaked, vagrant, predatory, tweaked, or worse—meek, diffident, doe-eyed, apologetic) and force herself to look directly into their eyes as she exited. Whatever she saw there, she discovered within herself a person who would know what to do next, a person who could smile or nod or stare back expressionless, a person who could be discarded when the moment was past and she was no longer needed.

This is how she becomes anything. Now she stares into the camera and tells herself a story.

"Yeah, baby," she says, shifting her hips. "Sure I like to party." She chews the words like meat in her mouth. This is the taste that slides down her throat: vinegar, sugar, whiskey, salt. These words are the potion that will transform her.

Everything disappears: the director's phone lit up and twitching against the sofa cushions; the crumpled napkin full of prosciutto; the assistant sighing deeply, bored, daydreaming; the coffee table full of half-empty water bottles, a different color of lipstick around the mouth of each bottle; the casting director dabbing at his nose with a tissue, the fever in his eyes and the rasp of his voice as he says "Go again"; the buzz of her own image pulsing on the video monitor . . .

"Yeah, baby," she repeats. She stares into the camera's single bulging glass eye. "Sure I like to party."

5

Birdie crosses the parking lot outside the casting studio. Where the asphalt meets the sidewalk is a pay phone, shaded by the leaves of a squat brown palm tree. She spies it from a distance and stands still for a moment. A slight breeze lifts her hair off her shoulders and the sun is warm and bright. Suddenly she is holding the receiver. Trash rustles at her feet— yellow and orange fast food wrappers, marked-up classifieds, an empty plastic soda bottle—until the updraft from a passing bus drags it all into the street.

She deposits the coins and dials the number. Mother once told her never to pick up the phone on the first three rings. It makes you seem desperate, she said, like you're just sitting around waiting for someone to call you. Like you have nothing better to do. And so when the phone would ring Mother would stare at the jangling receiver, counting the rings until she was certain that whoever was at the other end of the line would not think she needed them.

Four rings! Those four old rings, each longer than the last it seems, and then Mother answers. *Hello*, she says. It is a voice that will always be familiar. *Hello?* she says again, lifting the word into a question. Birdie won't speak. These are the sounds that she offers instead: the bus brakes squealing, its hydraulic doors gasping open, the bass booming out of an open car window, the squeak of the wheels on a homeless man's shopping cart, and his shouts of dissension as he debates himself. Also, Birdie offers the in and out of her breath as she imagines the room in which her mother stands, its wallpaper adorned with flowers and fruit, the ancient telephone the color of mustard, and the dim hallway stacked high with yellowed newspaper. Or perhaps she is in bed, propped up by pillows, her sleep mask pushed up onto her forehead, those painted eyes staring unblinking at the ceiling.

This is the gift that Birdie gives them, these calls from pay phones at the edges of parking lots. This is the gift she gives herself as well, so that she can believe that she is not so horrible after all. She is good not to make them wonder. Well, maybe not good, but perhaps a bit better.

Hello? the voice says again, getting softer, understanding. She is alive and they know it, far away and they know it. The line hisses with static. Birdie pushes the receiver down into its little silver holster. It is possible, someday, that she will say something, but she doesn't know what. Until then, the space of three hellos is what they get before she hangs up the phone.

She doesn't call Judah anymore. She called him once, back near the beginning, in that first year away. He said hello and waited as the phone line hissed and clicked. Then he said her name as a question: *Birdie?* She had the same question, whether it was actually her doing these things. She said nothing. Until that moment, she had not imagined him without her. But suddenly she saw it: Judah walking down the narrow hallway, Judah filling a glass with water from the kitchen faucet, Judah standing stunned in the light from the open refrigerator, the phone suddenly ringing on the wall behind him, making him jump, making him turn to it, making him wonder. He breathed and sighed and then she closed her eyes and dropped the pay phone back into its cradle. She was afraid he would say he forgave her. Judah was too certain, too good. No matter what she could have told him he would've said he understood.

She doesn't call Judah because there is no need for it. A year ago, she wrote a letter at Redmond's suggestion. In a moment of inebriation, she had confessed. *My husband*, she said, and then clapped her hand over her mouth. *For fuck's sake*, said Redmond. *Take care of it. Now, before you have any money.*

So she sent a proper letter to the county courthouse in Powhatan, Virginia. She needed, she wrote, the forms for divorce. She gave them names, dates, Social Security numbers, and Redmond's office as a return address.

The court's response arrived six weeks later, typed on county letterhead. She remembers reading the letter as she stood across from Redmond's desk. Dust sparkled in the air, rising, defying gravity. She remembers the black letters perched upon the thick ecru paper and, illuminated by the sunlight that glowed behind the page, the paper's watermark: a coat of arms featuring a dove nestled between tobacco leaves and, floating beneath it, the motto *Parmi Les Elus*. She does not remember the letter's words exactly and though she is certain it did not state the facts in this way, this is what she remembers, this is what it said: Judah is dead.

Redmond, she is certain, said that he was sorry. She is certain that he drove her home, she is certain he gave her a peach-colored pill and a swallow of water, she is certain he put her to bed. She is certain that he called the county and dug up the details and then recited them calmly as he sat in an armchair beside her bed. Carbon monoxide, as Judah slept. *Had you been there with him*, Redmond began, but he did not finish. There was no need to finish. *Lucky*, was all he said then, smoothing the hair from her forehead. She nodded. She knew she should be grateful but she could not grab on to the thought. The pill bloomed inside her, its smooth petals opening out, out, and she opened too, her head rolling across the pillow as Redmond explained how treacherous even the air can be, how poison can hang invisible over a sleeping body. She did not look at him. She examined the palm of her hand as he murmured: faulty ducts, faulty lines, slow leaks. Your breath is deeper when you sleep. Do you understand? *Yes*, she said, her voice slow and strange. Those lines on her palm, crossing back and forth, she wondered what they meant, what was possible to predict. She searched for the line that could have told her this. *Painless*, Redmond finally said softly in the darkness. *Yes*, she said again to hear the word. Then he cleared his throat and left.

Now she concentrates on other things: the squeal of ice cracking apart in her glass, the deepening lines at the corners of her eyes (she applies serum with her ring finger, the finger with the lightest touch, a makeup artist once told her, try to be gentle; this is her religion, turning back the clock), the individual letters in each word of a script. Words are better managed when reduced to their parts—lines, curves, abstractions; as they curl into each other, meaning wriggles through the cracks. Everywhere, meaning.

Judah lives in her dreams and so she tries not to sleep, not to dream. She is tired of meeting him in that blank white field. She is tired of him turning and running away from her. She had meant to run from him but maybe she never did. Maybe she died there with him, lying beside him on the bed, and this is the punishment for never loving him, not as she should.

This is the limbo where she waits for forgiveness. Someone will decide what she deserves. She listens to the ocean and stares at the sky and walks along hallways and pauses outside doors. She watches through glass walls, deciphering gestures. She overhears whispers, discerning motives. She swallows her questions. Her patience is boundless, her politeness compulsory. She smiles and listens and waits her turn. They tell her that she was great, really great. They avoid her eyes always but especially when they say thanks. Sometimes they say yes without meaning to (it is an impulse here, to lob a promise like a stone at her retreating figure) and retract it later in subsequent phone calls.

That night she lies awake in the humming darkness of her bedroom and remembers what Redmond said: that she is lucky. Other girls carry rabbit's feet, lockets, four-leaf clovers. They cross their fingers. No, luck is living through things. Just a little while longer, perhaps. She pulls these thoughts together and holds them close, like flowers against her chest, breathing air that could be poison in slow, shallow breaths.

6

"I'm having trouble hearing you," says Redmond. His voice is distant and Birdie can tell from its thinness that he is in his car, talking into his headset. "Hang on for a minute."

"Can you hear me?" Birdie shouts. She is sitting on the patio of her rented guesthouse, sipping scotch and staring across the lawn to the back of the main house. There is silence for a moment, a high metallic silence followed by a click and then a longer, duller silence. She hangs up and waits for him to call back. It is twilight and as darkness falls it is easy to see through the main house's sliding glass doors and into the living room—the shag of a flokati rug in the middle of the floor, the clear plastic bubble chair suspended from the ceiling by a silver chain, the Rothko hanging over the sofa, its reds and oranges merging into what seemed to be a pillar of fire.

As is nearly everything in her life, the guesthouse is something that Redmond arranged, a favor from a producer friend. In exchange for the cheap rent she keeps an eye on the main house, which the producer and his wife leave empty much of the time. *They hate renters*, Redmond said, and then clarified when he saw Birdie's expression. Main house renters, not guesthouse renters. A landscaping company tends the yard and the post office forwards the mail and a timer turns the lights on and off at the appropriate times, so there's not much left for Birdie to do except to stare at the back of the house and wish that she lived there, or rather wish that she could afford to live there, that she had the kinds of success that make such excess possible. The houses other people leave empty are nicer than anything she has ever occupied.

Her phone rings again and she picks it up without saying hello. "I'm roaming!" says Redmond. "I'm on fucking Olympic and I'm roaming. Listen. I got good feedback on you the other day on the hooker murder thing."

"Really?"

"Yeah. So we'll wait and see. You're in the running, whatever that means."

"In the running? Jesus. That's vague."

"You've got a scowl you can hear, did you know that? Don't be so negative. Anger is aging."

"Don't insult me into submission, okay? I can't stand that." She touches her face, consciously relaxing the muscles.

"Just a friendly reminder, my dear," Redmond says. "Honestly, I don't know what's going to happen on this one. Grant Minger is a volatile director. A genius, yes, but he has a reputation as being a bit of a tyrant. Listen, I have to run. All I can do is keep an eye on it. And I will." Then he says goodbye.

Most geniuses Birdie met were tyrants—it came with the territory. She had a way with tyrants (and geniuses) because she was angry, because she was uneducated, because she lied. It was all so very interesting to the kind of man who likes to understand everything. Also she was beautiful, which they rarely were—a borrowed currency they liked to spend. Her last genius was three years ago, an independent film director named Oscar of all things, a winner at Sundance slumming on a beer commercial in Vancouver. After three days she was tired of him, the way she was always tired of a man after she had slept with him. She couldn't stand the sight of him shuffling around his room in the plush hotel bathrobe, his pale white feet padding across the carpet. *You're a mystery,* he had sighed wetly against her neck. *Mystery is code for liar, as applied to a beautiful woman*, she said. *God*, Oscar said. *I love that.* If they were ever kind, and they sometimes were (though not Oscar, who drank the contents of the mini-bar and shoved her into the wall of his Vancouver hotel room when she said she hadn't seen his movie—*Who the fuck are you, anyway?* he had said, staggering back onto the bed as she slid down the wall. *Some neglected demographic?*), it was a wonderfully pleasant surprise. But she did not expect it.

Birdie throws her phone out onto the lawn where it perches on the freshly cut grass. She should go retrieve it but she doesn't want to. She thinks briefly of the screen direction for this scene: *Woman of questionable age sits, depressed and lethargic, in a lawn chair. She cannot muster the volition to stand up and retrieve her phone and so she stares at it, willing it to move. As always, her will is not enough. The phone remains in the grass, motionless. She takes a sip of her drink and resolves, as always, to straighten her messes in the morning.*

It is that time of day when everything is even, when the color of the evening is the color of her scotch: dark at the top, light at the bottom, toffee-tinted, sweet, dusky, deep, heavy, good. She sits there staring into the main house until the lights turn, automatically, off. She is left in darkness but her drink is sinking in so it's a good darkness, a soft and empty darkness, and she sits there for a long time.

7

Birdie first met Redmond at a party nearly six years ago. He had a different girlfriend then, a producer named Joy Wallace. He always seemed to have a girlfriend and although he generally seemed uninterested in them they were usually too self-involved to notice. Joy drove a Tiffany-blue '67 Rambler Rebel, suffered from obscure food allergies—because she hadn't been breastfed, she told anyone who would listen—and had an incontinent dog named Jamboree who went to weekly therapy. Joy's therapy was twice weekly, as were her enemas. Birdie knew all of this because Joy employed Birdie's then roommate, a girl named Beverly Halstead, as her personal assistant. Joy insisted upon calling Beverly Halstead "Beverly Hills." If Beverly didn't answer her cell phone, Joy would leave messages on the voice mail at their apartment. "Beverly Hills," she would say. "I'm desperate for a pair of Mathsson chaises for the patio. Help me, honey. I'm useless at these things." Joy wasn't useless at everything. She was a big shot at Framed Features and had lived for a long time in an enormous Tudor in Brentwood. She made a great point of being egalitarian enough to invite Beverly to her parties, although she also made a point of introducing Beverly as her assistant and treating her as such. Beverly spent most of her time at these parties tending to Joy's largely imagined emergencies—putting lower wattage bulbs in the light fixtures because everyone looked *bizarrely unattractive*; monitoring the volume of the stereo because it was *all thump-thump-thumpy*; singing a lullaby to Jamboree because he was *jumpy as a jackrabbit, the poor bunny!* Still, Beverly insisted upon going and on bringing Birdie with her. This was back when free food and drink were reason enough to do anything. Birdie and Beverly would bring purses so large they could only be called duffel bags and stuff them full of bottles of liquor and wine, crackers and cheese, olives, cured meats, anything that seemed expensive and portable. Birdie was in the pantry looking for Beverly's favorites—vanilla vodka and Wheat Thins—when Redmond stepped into the doorway.

"Like an alley cat," he said later. "You were rummaging. I watched you. You were stealing!"

"Not stealing," she said. "Pilfering."

When he asked her who she was, Birdie said "Nobody." Redmond thought it was the most charming thing he had ever heard. At least that is what he said at the time. *At last*, he had said. *Someone who admits it*.

At the time, he stood in the doorway of the pantry and ran his eyes along the length of her body, a gaze as brazen and deliberate as a hand slipping beneath her clothing. She leaned against the pantry shelves and closed her eyes, waiting for something to happen. She believed this moment could change things. "No," he said. "Look at me." So she did. She opened her eyes and looked directly at him. He reached toward her and touched a strand of her hair, arranging it just so against her shoulder. Then he pulled his hand away. "Get used to it," he said softly. "Stares from hideous strangers."

She laughed and bowed her head. She blushed. He wasn't hideous. He must have been about forty at the time, with the kind of face that would likely look the same for the next twenty-five years, squared off and suntanned, craggy in places, with a devilish mouth and a few lines around the eyes, a face that looked best squinting into sunlight. That is how he had looked at her then, as if she were a light source that blinded him. He stood squinting in the pantry doorway, offering her compliments one after another, and she gobbled them up, hungry as a bird. He asked her, "Is that how you got your name, little Birdie? Because you're so hungry?" Later, much later, Birdie realized that Redmond was referring to the need he saw in her—how reliant you are on a gaze, he once told her; actors exist only when you look at them—but at the time she thought he was referring to the duffel bag stuffed full of cheese and crackers. So she laughed and told him the story of how she actually got her name, how her mother was lying in a hospital bed right after delivery, holding her new baby in her arms, and looked up to see a bird sitting on the windowsill, tapping on the glass. "It's a bad omen, a bird at the window," Birdie told him. "It means someone in your family is going to die. So she named me Birdie. To appease the universe, I suppose." She pushed an arm outward, indicating the world. "True story," she added, because it *was* true, a point worth mentioning since most of her stories were not. Redmond laughed and went for an easy joke. He said that she was lucky her mother hadn't seen a dump truck.

It was this exchange and the conversation that followed that led to everything: the auditions and commercials and double work that had all seemed like a big deal at the time and now seemed like so much nothing. Redmond had never tried to sleep with her, a fact that used to seem like a compliment, the implication being that he knew she was too good for him. Her youth and promise were too palpable, gifts too precious to bestow on any old Joe. Now the implications of his restraint were changing: her promise was less palpable, her youth was less . . . young. There had been plenty of Joes. Redmond still squinted when he looked at her, but she suspected that she was no longer the sun. Now it was as if she were a cave painting, too primitive to hold any meaning for him beyond the obvious ones: here she is hunting, gathering, running. Sometimes when she spoke, she imagined he only heard a series of grunts. Not that it mattered. She had never really wanted him to sleep with her. She just wanted him to want to.

"Whatever happened to Joy?" Birdie once asked Redmond.

"She's a lesbian now. Not a fake one. The real deal. What ever happened to Beverly Hills?"

Beverly Hills had returned home to Washougal, Washington, later that year, where she could be Beverly Halstead again. Her parents promised to help pay for her apartment if she came home and she would also have the use of her father's old car. She was tired of Joy, anyway, and she was tired of pilfering vodka and crackers when in Washougal she could afford to buy them. When Beverly left she told Birdie, "I have a good feeling about this." Birdie knew she was referring to both of their futures.

The following year Beverly sent Birdie a letter. In it, Beverly said that she was doing just fine. She was working as a temp at an accounting firm and her apartment was kind of drab and the car kept breaking down—but still she insisted that it would all work out in the end. "I have a good feeling," she said again, in silly round letters. Birdie had read Beverly's letter on her patio, having just returned from a party. At the time the patio was new to her, as were Redmond's friends' parties, and she was giddy from the possibility that all of these new things seemed to offer. Reading Beverly's letter, she had wondered how someone could stay so positive about something when all signs seemed to indicate otherwise. She set the letter aside and made a cocktail and went back out to sit on her little patio. The haze of drink filled her with relief and gratitude that she was not Beverly Halstead, caught in the claustrophobic embrace of her family. She was not loved much by anyone, not anymore, but she had decided it was for the best. Love was a series of compromises that led to shitty jobs and dark apartments and broken-down cars.

Birdie stared across the dim yard into the main house and its quiet, glowing interior. Those beautiful rooms seemed to be her future: close and lovely and ready for occupancy. She decided not to reply to the letter that night. She intended to respond when she could tell Beverly everything had worked out in the end, just as she had predicted.

So there was a time when Redmond had seemed amazed by her and she by him. There was a time when the parts, however small, had not seemed silly. She screamed on a hilltop as a meteor approached, she sobbed into a handsome drifter's shoulder, she pulled a white shirt from the dryer and smiled into the camera. She bought shoes and wine with her deposited checks and she thought of this as progress.

Contrast. One night that previous spring, just after the Judah letter, Birdie came home from a party, went to her kitchen, filled a pot with water, and put it on the stove to boil. She was drunk and hungry and she was going to boil some spaghetti because that's all she had on hand. She was alone and went to the sofa to lie down. After a while she awoke to the shriek of the smoke detector. The house was filled with acrid black smoke. She was disoriented initially, running first to the front door, flinging it open to ventilate the house, and then suddenly remembering the stove. In the kitchen, a plume of smoke rose up, staining the ceiling with black clouds. The pot was boiled dry and scorched black, its plastic handle a molten lump. Birdie turned off the burner. She opened the back door and grabbed the pot with a dish towel and threw it into the yard where it lay in the grass, smoking like a cauldron. The smoke detector stopped wailing. She returned to the sofa and lay there, staring at the smoke stains on the ceiling, looking for a pattern.

She told Redmond the story later and he asked her, "What if you hadn't woken up?" He had sounded bored and she was bored too. He was tired of her self-pity. She was tired of other things, of waking up and of sleeping, of the sameness of her dreams, those usual terrors—Judah there and not there, Judah turning and running, Judah as only an outline of something—interrupted by a sudden awareness that none of it was real, that it would all disappear the moment she opened her eyes. That moment was supposed to be a relief, but it wasn't.

"Well?" Redmond persisted. This was his project ever since the Judah letter: to remind her of how lucky she was to be here, to be anywhere. He wanted her to admit it.

"But I did wake up," she said. Redmond sighed—he had wanted something different, but hers was the only relevant answer. She had woken up. She had, and she did, and she would.

8

"The best, worst, and only thing to know about Carine is this. She can take care of anything. Nothing fazes her, you can count on it. She would hide the bloody knife for you," says Redmond, eyes closed, leaning back in his deck chair. "Isn't that right, my darling?"

"Oh yes," says Carine, laughing, standing behind Redmond and rubbing his neck, her stacks of gold bangles flashing in the sun. "Just tell me where it is and I'll take care of it." A former production assistant, Carine is now at Paramount working in publicity. "My Paramount paramour," Redmond calls her. Her sole personal quality seems to be efficiency. Within minutes of Birdie's arrival at Redmond's house Carine has procured drinks for each of them, herded them onto the pool deck, popped open the sun umbrellas, brought out a stack of towels, and turned on the stereo. Now the bass throbs and trembles, sending tiny vibrations across the surface of the swimming pool.

"I'll remember that," says Birdie. "Unless, of course, it's my blood, your knife."

"Oh, the conspiracies against you!" sighs Redmond, opening his eyes and reaching for a magazine.

If she lets her eyes defocus, as she does now, Birdie sees a double of everything: two shirtless Redmonds reading *Variety*; two caftan-clad Carines, massaging Redmond's four shoulders and nuzzling his two heads with her two noses; two kidney-shaped swimming pools, full of still, clear water; two pulsing suns wobbling toward the horizon; two glasses of scotch in her own two right hands; twenty black-painted toenails peeking out from under two large plaid afghans.

Carine stands suddenly, stripping down to a metallic bathing suit and kicking her sandals under her lounge chair. Her skin is so pale it is nearly translucent, blue with veins and misted with freckles. As she slathers zinc oxide over her face and along her arms and legs, her stacks of bangles clack together. The sunscreen doesn't fully absorb, coating her skin in a chalky white layer that leaves her looking undead, a whippet-thin Lazarus in Jackie O sunglasses stepping toward the bright water of the swimming pool. She bends down to touch its surface. The gold bracelets and the oversized sunglasses and the name Carine and the vaguely glamorous but low-level job seem to imply a life spent at leisure. As Birdie watches Carine she thinks of her aunts. If she met them now she wonders if she would hate them as she instantly hated Carine, as she finds herself hating, sometimes unwillingly, all subsidized women. She tells herself it isn't jealousy that she feels, but rather allegiance to a work ethic.

"Come swim," Carine says. As she wades into the pool she coils her hair up on top of her head and secures it with a single oversized hairpin.

"It's too cold," says Birdie, shivering under her blanket.

"I love it," says Redmond. "It's seventy-four degrees. You're like a greyhound."

"Are you sick?" Carine asks.

"No. Redmond knows what's wrong with me. I'm just tired and grumpy."

"A chronic condition," says Redmond.

"You know I have to ask again. What's happening with the hooker murder thing? I thought I had a shot."

"You probably do, when and if they get their financing

sorted out. It's a mess over there. What did you hear, Carine darling?" he calls toward her. He turns back to Birdie. "I love her grapevine. It's less discreet than mine."

Carine is treading water at the far end of the pool. "Some issue with the backers," she shouts, breathless. "They don't like Minger. He's one moody motherfucker. He threatened to piss on the latest script. Like, he actually *took it out*. Plus, I guess there's another hooker murder thing. I mean, there's *always* another hooker murder thing. But it's Maggie Mayo and she's so fucking expensive. Ever seen her rider? It's all Gulfstreams and Reiki masters. They might not get financing for both projects."

"God, don't tell me this stuff. I cannot hear about Maggie Mayo's absurd requirements," Birdie says, covering her eyes with her palms. "I'm just sitting here. Shriveling away."

"Use some of Carine's sunblock." Redmond looks over at her. "Actually, don't. You would look good with some color."

"Shit! Redmond, I am perfect for that part."

"Bird, you'd be great but let's not overstate it. The hooker's alive for all of five minutes. Five nude minutes."

"Honestly. You know it's a great part, Redmond."

"I do. I know. It's sensational. Five nude minutes that you'd know what to do with. But until it happens it's not a consideration."

"Shit," says Birdie, burrowing farther down into her blanket.

Carine is paddling back to the shallow end of the pool. Her lips are blue. "It's a little cold," she says, stepping up out of the water.

"Well, grab a towel, darling. You weigh sixty-seven pounds," says Redmond. "Carine, say something positive to Birdie. I'm too exhausted. Where's that guy with big teeth when you need him?"

"Birdie, come to my housewarming tomorrow, it will be fun," says Carine, toweling the water from her body.

"Come on," says Redmond. "Big teeth? *Changes lives?*" He sighs.

In a single seamless motion Carine pulls her caftan over her head and unfastens her wet swimsuit, letting it fall to the ground. She lies back in her deck chair and says in a sing-song, "We'll have mi-mo-sas . . ."

"Bingo," says Redmond. "Birdie speaks mimosa. Fluently."

Birdie pretends not to hear them. She lets her eyes defocus again as Redmond and Carine murmur back and forth. She imagines walking to the edge of the pool and staring down into it, then letting herself fall in and sink to the bottom. She would like to lie down there for a while, where all of this chatter would be muffled into low, hollow tones. It might be so peaceful she would just decide to stay. Not to worry. If she drowned today, efficient Carine would take care of it. She would drag Birdie up out of the water and try a few chest compressions, Yurman bracelets jangling, then sob briefly into Redmond's shoulder before placing the necessary phone calls.

Back in Vancouver, after her run-in with Oscar, Birdie returned to her hotel room and filled the enormous marble bathtub with water. She stripped naked and slid into the bath and sat there for a long time, the water turning cold as a fantasy of drowning played out in her mind. It was revenge that she wanted—for Oscar to stand outside the door to her hotel room, confused and belligerent, angry at her lateness, and then finally fall silent as the medics pushed past him with her body, stiff and still and wrapped in white sheets. Perhaps later the moment he had shoved her into the wall would replay in his mind and keep him awake. Maybe she would haunt him, maybe he would suffer, or maybe not. Maybe he would sleep, dreamlessly. She was one girl with one line in one beer commercial. *A bikini-holder*, Oscar had teased. Even worse: at the time he said it, it had felt like a compliment. No, he would not blame himself, not with words like *crazy* and *struggling* and *actress* at his disposal. The truth, whatever that might be, would not come out, and even if it did what kind of news was it—one person hurting another?

"Birdie!" says Redmond.

"What?" she whispers, drowsy from the sun, the drink, the memory. She does not know which Redmond to look at: there are two of them, gesturing with a magazine.

"Did you even hear me? I said we knew it was inevitable," said Redmond, brandishing *Variety*. "Melena: The Sequel."

When Birdie leaves Redmond's she does not go home. Instead she drives up into the Hollywood Hills, toward the street where she remembers attending the party at Melena Duvall's house. It is nightfall. Soon Birdie is crawling around the curves of Mulholland Drive and on up its steep, dark switchbacks until the twinkling lights of the city become visible through the vegetation. There, glinting beyond the hushed green-black trees, the city lights appear enchanted, and the houses nestled beside them, behind sloping brick walls and wrought-iron gates and towering hedges, seem charmed too, tucked away from the ugliness and chaos of the city below by the spell of a good witch, one whose primary power is aesthetics. Oh, the good and lucky children tucked into these beds, their sleeping rosebud lips pursed into a kiss for the witch that got them here. And their mummies and daddies float across their patios, fire pits lit and burning, toasting their good fortune.

The piece in *Variety* was "Melena Duvall Goes Home." Redmond read it to Birdie by the swimming pool as she lay immobile under her afghan, as she sucked the scotch off her ice cubes, as the sun went down. "The independent film *Where I'm From*, produced by Albert Dave and Juliette Miller of Serious Pictures, tells the story of Libby Bishop, a Southern girl who, after leaving home and struggling to succeed in the big city, goes back home to confront her demons. With plans to begin shooting in South Hill, Virginia, next month, Miller tells us she believes this will be the role that lands Duvall awards-show gold."

That was all—a blurb, a horoscope—that told them virtually nothing and also everything. Now they will wait for the call to come, asking for Birdie to stand in for Melena, and she will take it because there is nothing else on the horizon, not the hooker murder thing, nothing viable. They will wait and say yes and be Thankful for the Opportunity.

Bougainvillea and palm fronds and eucalyptus and blooming vines blanket the landscape. In the dark perfumed air, crossing Birdie's headlights as she pulls to a stop in front of Melena's house, flower petals drift like falling snow. Clay-red terra-cotta tiles undulate across the roof, dropping away to thick white walls swirled with plaster. The effect is of a house made of candy—marshmallow walls and a licorice roof—insubstantial but good enough to eat.

Birdie sits in her car watching the house. It is like wanting someone else's husband, noting the veins on the backs of his hands and mapping their path along his forearms, hungry for the details of his body. The house, the life, the parties, the parts, all of it belongs to Melena Duvall. In this moment, Birdie imagines that she will always be this way, on the outside of everything lovely, effortless, safe. If there is only room for one of them, one girl who came from nothing who looks like this, Melena Duvall has already taken it. Melena Duvall, with her infinity pool and her crystal shoes and her early buzz and her famous fucks, locked away in her candy castle like some coked-up Cinderella.

It is good to admit these things. It is good to sit here in the dark confines of her dented blue car, outside of everything, so close to what could be but still out of reach. Melena's gates sit closed and quiet and the night smells like the nape of a lovely young neck. Flower petals drift in the air as if moved by breath.

This is how it will be. Birdie will stand exactly where Melena will stand, as she has before, with the light in her eyes. "Look there," the assistant director will say, indicating her eye line. And she will look *there*, for what feels like forever, into the empty space where he points his finger. She will stand there motionless as the lights move around her. In her peripheral vision, grips and electricians and set dressers and production assistants will mill around, murmuring, carrying things. The camera will search her face for the perfect balance of darkness and light, an opportunity for radiance, the sweetest frame, so that when Melena arrives they can go right away, she will stand right in place, she will not waste any of her time.

9

On the plane back from Vancouver, the trip for Oscar's beer commercial, a man seated beside Birdie began praying.

"I'm nervous," he had said as he took his seat beside her. "I hate to fly."

"Don't be," said Birdie. "It will be fine."

He smiled, but when the plane began to move he closed his eyes and held his open palms in front of his face as if he were holding a book. This was right before takeoff and his lips moved silently, forming words she could not hear.

Soon the plane began to rumble down the runway. Birdie could not help but watch the man beside her. As the plane gained speed, so did his lips. She remembers what he was wearing because it was so ordinary—khaki pants and a blue dress shirt and a wedding band glinting gold against his pale finger and a cheap-looking tie adorned with a pattern of grapevines; only the godless have a sense of style, it seems—making him appear all the more ordinary, just an ordinary man in an ordinary wardrobe, on his way home from selling sprockets in some Vancouver office park, praying to his ordinary God. As she looked at him, she saw in a flash the twilight horrors of suburban streets and yards, the bicycles swooping in slow arcs like carnivorous birds, the cars creeping along the asphalt, their headlights drawn to the inevitable houses lodged like teeth in the dark mouth of the neighborhood. She had wished past this already, past the gravity of culs-de-sac and their predictable cast, the fathers mowing the lawns and making love to the mothers, the mothers piloting the station wagons and feeding the children, the children eating their dinners and then stopping to scream, their doughy fingers balled into fists, the taste of milk turning sour in their mouths, their small gray minds suddenly aware of how much there is above them, of all that is hovering just out of reach. She was not a part of anything he was a part of, not anymore—she did not believe what he believed or need what he needed or love what he loved—she knew this just by looking at him. And yet, as she watched the man's mouth in an effort to decipher what he might be saying, she thought for a moment that she understood, that she knew what he was asking for and she wanted it too. This was a hope they could share: the desire to live through this. As they surged forward and lifted into the air, as the clouds parted and fell past the windows, as they moved, ostensibly, closer to heaven, the man closed his eyes and gripped his armrests and repeated a single word. Another request for safety, he was saying *please please please*.

10

"I died once. For seventeen seconds," this person named Lewis insists, shaking the ash from his cigarette into one of Carine's bamboo planters.

Redmond had said there might be opportunities at Carine's housewarming brunch. "People to meet," he had promised. But he always says that. Instead, there is a sea of other underemployed actors, avoiding the muffins, sucking down Bloody Marys, and eyeing each new party arrival. The power contingent is paltry: Redmond and a handful of Carine's current and former coworkers clustered together in the living room, shoulder to shoulder, chatting conspiratorially. Carine buzzes around the buffet table, replenishing the booze and rearranging the baked goods. And there is Lewis, a boy of maybe twenty, who recognized Birdie from a fabric softener commercial she did a few years ago and who was, pathetically, impressed. He is wearing a too-small suit and striped shirt and knit tie, the kind favored by English professors. He looks like a student from a boarding school farce, sent to Los Angeles in a sort of cultural exchange program. Somewhere in New England would be his counterpart, giving the stuffed shirts fits: a dude in a dining hall wearing board shorts and eating chicken with his fingers.

"Hmmm," says Birdie, sipping her Bloody Mary. "Wow."

"I know!" Lewis says. "It was crazy."

"Totally," she says, staring past him into the living room. Redmond is laughing too loudly, a sign that he too is miserable. This at least gives her some satisfaction.

"It was like I was outside of my own body," Lewis says, pressing his palms to his chest. "And I realized I'd never thought about it before. The end, you know. What happens on the other side, what's waiting for us? Is it heaven? Is it nothing?"

"I don't know," says Birdie, suddenly serious. She hasn't thought about this in a long time. In fact, in the last seven years, she counts the fact that she does not think about heaven anymore as her only major accomplishment.

"Did I tell you that I was surrounded by light?" he continues. "And I realized none of this matters. None of this Hollywood bullshit, getting famous and whatnot. I mean, I'm gonna see how it goes, the acting thing. But I'm not gonna get hung up on it. Because what matters, you know, is your spirit. You have to be ready for whatever comes next." He looks off into space longingly, as if waiting for a bus to arrive.

Birdie watches Lewis for a moment. He is in possession of a body that would have been carved into marble by now if people still did that sort of thing. She imagines his chest beneath his shirt as a lean stretch of ridges she could climb like a rock wall. The effect of the too-small suit is a desire to remove it—like a present wrapped in newspaper, one must rip past the nonsense to get to the goodies inside. His face is nearly perfect, its only flaw a slight lack of symmetry. The result is a preoccupied look, which lends him an air of depth that cannot possibly be deserved. Suddenly Birdie has an impulse to upset him, to tamper with his expression.

"If heaven is what matters, and it was right in front of you, why didn't you just go in? Why come back here, where you might fuck it all up?" she says, rearranging the celery stalk in her drink. She takes another deep pull from it. "Sorry, just being devil's advocate, but following your logic, you should have died."

A wisp of sadness passes over his face, occupying his eyes

and setting his lips into a line. There is pleasure in this, in watching the question rearrange his expression. Sometimes she just needs to know she can have an effect on somebody. He grasps her hand suddenly. "Sometimes," he says, searching her face for a reaction, "sometimes I wish I had."

11

It was a mistake to sleep with Lewis. The thought occurs to Birdie as he lies next to her speaking softly, and the thought forms so suddenly and distinctly that she fears she has spoken it out loud.

At Carine's, as the afternoon dwindled, she had found herself growing tired. She nearly nodded off in one of the oversized chairs flanking the fireplace. She was bored with the party; everyone seemed loud and greedy and unattractive, braying like mules with counterfeit laughter, milling around Carine's trough of a buffet table, eyeing the food hungrily but refusing to eat. No wonder. They were cannibals, all of them. Finally, Lewis offered to drive her home. "Because you seem tired," he had said, but the nature of the transaction was understood and she did not mind. The party had left her empty and she needed company.

There is a moment with a man, always, when she thinks of Wes, or rather of what changed in her when she was with him. The static in her mind is quieted for a time, the thoughts swarming like fireflies dart off into the darkness and without their light she is invisible. What a relief it is to disappear.

With Lewis, it was a moment when her appreciation of him temporarily superseded the disgust she felt for her own need. He leaned over her, whispering things, but she wasn't listening. She watched instead his beauty, the stranger moving in a blur above her: the edge of his cheekbone, the hollow of his mouth, the sloping trench of his hips. His arms coiled around her like snakes and she hoped for a moment that he would crush her, that he would grind her bones to powder. She closed her eyes, ready for death. Yet she lived.

Afterward, Lewis continued to speak dreamily about immortality. He theorized that heaven is a place where essentially everyone went and that hell is just a fictitious boogeyman that God provides to keep us in line. The real bastards, he said, Nazis and child molesters and certain key Republicans, don't go to hell. They just stay dead. When Birdie asked Lewis how he knew this he murmured, *Instinct*.

Acting is a way to die without dying, Lewis told her. You can leave yourself behind, inhabit stories that are not your story, have memories that are not your memories, and live lives that are not your life—all of those little suicides! He tried it for real once and emerged alive, with long raised scars along the insides of his arms and a memory of that glimpse of heaven. After his failed attempt, his mother took him to a Jungian analyst who told him that acting was a brilliant compromise.

Lewis went on to discuss his parents' expectations of him and the feeling that he was falling short in their eyes. His father was a sports-car-obsessed lawyer and his mother was a real estate agent, a Power Seller, divorced from each other but both still living in San Diego. They were impatient for him to succeed. The fact that he had not yet landed anything, even commercial work, weighed heavily on his mind. "You're lucky," he said. "You've done that"—referring again to the fabric softener commercial he had seen with the kind of reverence that should be reserved for *The Godfather*.

Birdie was silent during all of this talk and he did not seem to notice. At one point he decided they should have some water but he did not ask her to get it. He got up out of bed and pattered into her kitchen, quickly locating glasses that he filled from the faucet and brought back to the bedroom. *One for you and one for me*, he said upon returning.

Soon he turned to the subject of his younger brother who had died in an accident when Lewis was six and the brother, Gus, was three. The boy drowned in their swimming pool and Lewis felt he should've been watching more closely, especially since even then he had sensed that their mother was drinking too much, too early in the day. She often spent the whole day in her bathrobe back then, before Gus's death and the divorce and her new career as a real estate agent.

"I should've been watching," Lewis said quietly. "I was only six, but I was mature for my age." He went on to describe finding the boy's body floating facedown in the water. At first, he thought it was a toy.

It is during his soliloquy that Birdie realizes her mistake. She does not want to know about Lewis's search for a purpose, or what it was that he missed about San Diego, or what happened at the moment of his nondeath, or what the Jungian analyst told him, or any of the other ordinary, horrifying details of his life. She does not want to picture his brother's small body floating on the surface of the water in his little white shirt and little red shorts, and she does not want to know that the thick white scars that run along Lewis's forearms mark his own attempt at forgetting. Each new revelation adheres to her brain like a barnacle. She can't stand it, any of it. Her own uncertainty is too much, clawing at the doors of the rooms she shuts it in, resisting applications of logic and tumblers full of scotch, always squirming up from the dark to break the surface of any good moment. No, she cannot manage more.

"I don't know," Lewis murmurs, reaching for her.

"I can't," she says suddenly, pulling away and folding her arms across her chest.

"What is it?" he says. He is tucked snugly under the covers.

His expression is still open and unguarded and suddenly she can see what he must have looked like as a boy. He *is* a boy. He looks at her, wanting to understand.

"I'm sorry," she says, standing, pulling back the covers. "You have to leave."

"Okay," he says, confused. He gets up out of the bed and fumbles around on the floor for his clothes. "I thought you wanted me to stay."

"No," she says, her voice growing loud and unfamiliar. She grabs at the blankets, smoothing them frantically.

"I'll help," he says, reaching toward the bed. The low yellow glow of the bedside lamp quivers, illuminating his chest in such a way that she can see the contours of his ribcage beneath his skin, its gentle curves rising and falling a little more quickly than before because he is startled. His breathing has changed. She imagines his red heart like a clenched fist shaking inside his chest and in this moment she feels like a monster, but it's better like this, this way he'll want to forget her.

"No, don't help me," she says, looking toward him, but not at his face, she doesn't want to see his expression. She concentrates on his neck, the blue vein that throbs just along his Adam's apple. She says, "You have to understand. I won't be able to sleep. I need to have my bed a certain way."

She makes the bed, tucking in the corners and smoothing down the sheets. Headlights from the alley pass through her bedroom window. Lewis is leaving. She sits on the edge of the bed and feels the lights sweep over her body. Then they turn away, leaving her in the dark.

Alone again. The room seems battened with cotton, the sound of her breath folding into the soft white silence of her bedroom as soon as it leaves her lungs. She runs her fingers over the knots of chenille that repeat across the bedspread in shabby fleur-de-lis. The covers are still warm from their bodies.

She closes her eyes and decides what will come next: walking down the hallway and then on into the kitchen. In the kitchen is the cupboard and in the cupboard is the glass and in the freezer is the ice and in the pantry is the scotch and if she puts the scotch in the glass and the ice in the scotch the drink will grow cold in her hand. The ice will pop and snap, as familiar as a friend, and she will whisper to it, *Yes? What are you trying to tell me?* She'll listen for a moment to that breaking-apart sound. She'll press her lips against the glass and be cold for just a minute, and then she'll take a sip and feel warm again.

12

She is digging a hole in this dream and this dream is a memory.

She was a child, maybe seven years old. The hole was meant to be to China but she never quite made it there. The vine-choked red clay just wouldn't give and she only got about a foot down before she began hitting stones and the roots of trees. Mother watched Birdie dig from her bedroom window, hovering against the blinds until the sun sank below the tree line and it was time for dinner. Around the table, the distance to China was discussed with great specificity, along with details regarding the temperature of the earth's core. On the kitchen wall was a clock in the shape of an apple core and Birdie wondered if the earth's core was similar—studded with black seeds like teardrops. Mother said the task was fruitless, which meant that she would never get there, and which also seemed to indicate no apple seeds. Father said the task was dangerous, because of the stones and the sharp end of the shovel. Birdie nodded. After that, she was watchful. Below her feet, sometimes, the earth seemed to tremble. She knew now that the earth was not solid all the way down. Inside it shifted and boiled. Soon she abandoned the project entirely, out of fear that she either would or would not hit the hot center of the earth. After a few months' worth of rains, the hole eroded and filled in.

In her dream, the hole is not in her yard in Powhatan, Virginia—it has followed her here to Venice. This hole is deeper than the other one; is Time a spade that digs at the holes you start? She lies on her belly and peers down into it, straining to see something besides darkness. There is something small and glinting like silver in murky water. Something winks or smolders deep at the bottom.

In the corner of her eye there is movement: the neighbor's window shade? No, there is no one, but she feels eyes upon her, low and near. Suddenly she is afraid of the hole's gravity—that glinting silver thing is her wish, pulling her toward it—and she feels certain that she will disappear inside. Her belly slides along the dirt and her hands grab at nothing as she is drawn down into darkness.

Birdie wakes from the dream in a twist of sweat-soaked sheets, clawing at the spiderwebs in her eyes, choking on the dirt in her mouth, until she coughs and sits upright. These are only memories: the vines that covered the ground, the swing set, the little playhouse, the bicycle left in the yard. Green crept over every surface, every little plaything, until the bicycle was unridable, and the swings were all unswingable, and the playhouse was unplayable, its door bound shut with knotted vines. Daddy longlegs tiptoed along the dew-covered porch and bees fussed around the honeysuckle bushes like bridesmaids and pollen swirled in the air around her, powdery and star-colored and sparkling like galaxies. Everything crept and floated and grew. Snakeskins hung from the rafters of the toolshed, milky silver, ribbed from the spines that once thrashed inside them. They had seemed like ghosts hovering above her, the living part of them excised. When their skins got too small, they left them behind.

Birdie gets up out of bed and walks to the back door of her house. Through its window she sees the dim yard as it always is: manicured, undisturbed. The jagged silhouettes of plants shine green-black in the darkness. In the house across the way there is no sign of life.

Birdie goes to the bathroom to get a Xanax from the

medicine cabinet. She has been to a psychiatrist only once, after the Judah letter, to ask for something to help her sleep. Dr. Able had refused to give it to her—talk therapy, she said, should be where they started, let's go back to the beginning— but Birdie never went back. Xanax could be gotten from production assistants, teamsters, makeup artists. No need to plumb the depths for a couple of lousy pills. She locates the tablets she keeps in an old Advil bottle, pops one into her mouth, then cups water into her hands from the faucet and swallows it.

When she looks back up into the mirror she sees that her face is puffy from sleep and the effect is that she looks younger: plump, unlined, naïve, almost as young as Lewis. Almost. She presses her palms to her cheeks and blinks. This resembles the face that reflected back from Wes's mirror, its youth and its hunger illuminated by the bare bulb of the ceiling fixture, the face he plucked like a flower from a row in the movie theater.

Her stomach spins. She is remembering the playground, how she lay back on the whirligig's round metal platform, her body like a spoke stretched from the center to its edge. The sky sagged above them, pinned at the corners and heavy with stars. Wes grabbed on to the whirligig's edge and began to push so that it turned, faster and faster, until he was running, and Birdie felt her body begin to slide outward, pulled by centrifugal force. *Hang on*, he panted, running around and around, and so she hung on, her arms linked through the rails, the smells of grease and metal mixing with the smells of dirt and gin and trees and skin, gravity grabbing at her like quicksand as she reached for Wes, his laughing mouth a star, as the sky glittered, the wheel turned, the vault opened, and out she tumbled, emerging from darkness into other darkness, darkness without walls or corners, darkness that stretched always outward, soft as velvet, open and infinite.

The name of the movie she does not remember. It had something to do with love. But it is all the same anyway: the drinks, the night, the kisses, the boy, and later herself, reflected in the mirror. All of it was what she wanted to be rather than what was.

Birdie goes back to her bedroom to find her bed as she left it, ravaged from her nightmare. She tries to remake it, smoothing the sheets and refolding the corners, but she is too exhausted. The night and the walls crowd around her. She cannot get it right. So she wraps herself in a blanket and lies down on the hardwood floor. There in the dark she imagines the molten center of the earth rumbling just below the floorboards. Silver snakeskins hang from the ceiling. She feels the pill dissolving inside her, its little particles like stars entering her bloodstream. She feels the whirligig spin beneath her, the gravity of its circle as it pulls her out, out, out of her head into deep and dreamless sleep.

13

The following morning Birdie does not go to the gym. She does not shower or answer the ringing telephone. She stays inside with the shades drawn, curled on the sofa, watching the *Oceans Gone Wild* marathon on the nature channel, program after program about killer sea creatures. Cannibalistic squid grapple with each other's endless tentacles, shooting clouds of ink into the already murky ocean. A moray eel winds like a snake through the water, his jaw yawning wide in an expression of perpetual surprise. He hides beneath a bank of coral and waits there, grinning. A lone diver observes sharks from the confines of a steel cage lowered deep into the water. He speaks into his diving suit microphone. *This is wild*, he keeps saying. The microphone captures his quickening breath. The sharks circle the cage slowly and knock against the bars with their noses, their flat black eyes unblinking. *God, this is wild*.

She ignores the message from Redmond, his low perverted chuckle and then, "Why, you dirty, dirty girl. I can't take you anywhere. You have to tell me. No, don't tell me. But God, tell me. What was he? Nineteen? Let's buy him a tricycle. A red one! Call me. It's settled. I'm taking you to more parties."

She ignores, too, the other message, the one that wasn't really a message but five seconds of silence. Stingrays flap like vampire bats along the ocean floor as she presses the telephone to her cheek and listens. In the phone's static she hears breathing and she is certain it belongs to Lewis, sweet, beautiful Lewis, unable to ask but wanting to know, if there was something already wrong with her when he met her or if it was something that he had done.

14

Prior to the visit to Dr. Able and the request for Xanax, Birdie had noticed little things changing, lodging themselves in her consciousness, and asserting themselves in the most mundane ways.

First, she could never be satisfied that the bed was made properly. She would stretch the sheets taut, folding tight hospital corners and neatly tucking the fabric around the perimeter of the bed. Then she would lay a thin cotton blanket over top of it, making sure to keep equal lengths extending over each side of the mattress, smoothing the blanket as she tucked it so that it was free of wrinkles. Then she would lay out the duvet with equal precision, again keeping every side even in length. Finally, she would position the pillows, open ends of the pillowcases always facing out, at the head of the bed. But there was always something off, it seemed, a bump or a crooked corner, so that she would have to go back to the beginning, to start over. She could not sleep in the bed unless it was perfect. But when it was perfect, she did not want to ruin it. So she would fold down the covers carefully and evenly and slide into the bed with precision, and once she was in bed she would not move. She would lie on her back, silent and immobile, imagining that she was playing someone dead or paralyzed to assure herself of absolute stillness. Being completely motionless required such effort that she would eventually drop off into sleep.

Also, there were memories of things that hadn't seemed

important at the time and even now seemed quite ordinary—a certain bridge she drove over once in Saluda, Virginia, on her way to a revival (the town smelled like sulphur from a paper mill there and the surface of the bridge had ridges that thudded beneath the tires of the car, jostling her as if she were running over bodies); the camel crickets in her parents' basement (they would be hidden in the black and blue paisley pattern of the carpet until she stepped off the final stair and then the pattern would come alive, the crickets leaping out in every direction, two or three at a time, brazen, terrifying); the sound of Judah's footsteps in the hallway (she could tell if he had lost something by their stopping and starting, their advancing and retreating, and when he had found whatever it was, their quietly disappearing).

Sometimes these memories would be daydreams, and sometimes they would appear in her dreams. She would wake abruptly, fearful that she had run over a body, fearful that if she moved a camel cricket would leap up from the darkness, fearful that she would hear a voice from beyond her bedroom door, Judah's voice, looking for something that he had lost. Reality always took a few moments to settle in, at which time she would realize that those things were in Virginia, a long time ago, and though initially she would be relieved, she never really felt comforted.

Sometimes when she crosses a street she crosses slowly, testing her luck, tempting the oncoming traffic to speed up and hit her. It feels like a miracle when she reaches the other side. Cars sweep by behind her, the draft sends her hair flying, and for a moment she feels grateful. Her hands shake from the victory.

Each thought bobs up like a buoy, up out of the deep. Each thought is like a cricket, chirping while she tries to sleep.

"I can't sleep," she told Dr. Able. "It's stressful, this business." But Dr. Able had not given her the Xanax. Dr. Able had looked at her with her mournful, liquid brown eyes and jotted down a little note in her notebook and said that she was sorry. Dr. Able had wanted details, but details are exactly the problem.

15

"So I assume you know why we're having lunch," Redmond says. "I got the call. And not about the hooker murder thing."

"Let me guess. Melena?" Birdie says.

"Yes, our benefactor. *Where I'm From* is definitely happening. They want to meet you." Redmond snaps a breadstick in half with a flourish. He chooses the smaller half and gnaws on it enthusiastically.

"Meet me? She's already worked with me."

"The director wants to see you. A new guy, Max Mason. Fresh out of film school, his first big gig."

"Oh, great. Amateur hour."

"What if everybody thought that way?" He gestures at her with the gnawed-on end of his breadstick. "What chance would you have?"

"I'm not a beginner. I'm unsuccessful. There's a difference, though I'm not sure it's one that I want to think about."

"Well, I think you should meet with him. You're cultivating a relationship. Even though I have reservations, same as you."

She runs her finger around the platinum rim of her barren bread plate. "'Reservations' is an understatement of what I'm feeling right now," she says.

"I don't doubt it. This is a transitional time, Birdie. It's tough but you can push through it. My girl. My strong girl," he says, chewing. He pats her hand and takes a sip of water. "Now. The boy. The Montessori student. Talk to me."

"Please," she says. "Let me forget it."

"Oh, dear," says Redmond, wincing. "Does he adore you?"

"Maybe," she says. "Why?" She smiles and tilts her head back. "Jealous?"

Redmond considers this. "Always," he says. He holds her gaze for a moment and then he looks away, turning his attention to the other half of the breadstick. He begins to break it into bits. "Though I suppose I should be relieved. So far, my sense of self-preservation has kept me out of the meat grinder that is your love life."

"Self-preservation? Please. My locked door is what's keeping you out of my love life." She takes a drink from her glass.

Redmond laughs. "Oh, there's a lock? Well. Honestly, I'm surprised there's a *door.* I pictured it as more of a *lobby.*" His hands sweep outward, indicating an expanse as wide as their table.

"You picture it?" Her eyes travel to his. "Interesting."

Redmond glances down at his bread plate and shakes his head. "If you gave me as much credit as you give yourself . . ."

"I wouldn't call it credit. Don't you know bravado when you see it, Redmond? Don't go mistaking me for someone who is satisfied."

"Oh, there is no danger of that. Listen, I'm not asking you to be satisfied. I'm asking you to be grateful."

Her expression falters. She leans toward him and lowers her voice. "I am, Redmond. I know you have your work cut out for you. I know I am *withering* on the vine." She knew how it went. Girls become women. They fudge the numbers, make some adjustments, and are tolerated for the littlest while. Then everyone is in a meeting one day and it comes down to the beautiful woman or the beautiful girl. According to Oscar, his decision to cast her in the beer commercial was based largely on the opinion of three production interns from UCLA. He showed them a table full of headshots and said, *Okay, fellas, who would you rather fuck?* Two of the three pointed at her picture. When she recoiled at the story, Oscar was genuinely surprised. *It's a compliment,* he told her. *The interns won't want to fuck you forever.*

"Don't be dramatic. Boy toy aside, you're not exactly Norma Desmond. According to my own calculations, you're twenty-six. And going nowhere, as you call it, is at least paying your bills. You don't seem to realize it could be a lot worse. That could be you"—he indicates the approaching waitress—"bringing you your lunch. But no." Redmond pauses as the waitress arrives with their salads. He shoos away her offer of the pepper mill and continues. "You've got a hot little bod and SAG health insurance. For chrissake, you have *dental*. There are opportunities out there, but your attitude is a self-fulfilling prophecy."

"So everything is my fault."

"No. But you radiate dissatisfaction like a white-hot sun. Is that helping?" He takes a large bite of salad. "Just stop with your wounded thing. God, it's worse than your bitter thing."

In moments like this, it is easy to hate Redmond—his imperviousness to criticism, his ease in assessing everyone, including her. "Don't order wine. It's lunch," he had said when they first arrived. Then he had sighed. "Or go ahead and order it. Do what you want." She ordered a scotch and soda just to spite him.

"It's not a wounded *thing*," Birdie says. "I *am* wounded." She smacks the table with her open palm, sending a vibration along the table, clattering the silverware and the china and the ice in their glasses.

Redmond glances around the restaurant at the turned faces, startled by the sound. Their necks seem mechanical, twisting toward them in unison. Redmond smiles, spears a leaf of endive on his fork, and holds it in front of his mouth.

He says through his grin, "Laugh like you said something funny." Then he throws back his head and laughs, shoulders shaking, and she laughs too until the startled faces return, one by one, to their plates. When asked to play along, this is what you do.

16

On certain days, when it is too hard to be alone, Birdie walks up to the beach and lets herself be pulled into the stream of people that rush along the boardwalk. This is not Hollywood. These are ropy-haired surfers, tanned and salt-crusted, eyeing the tide. These are potheads, made hungry by daylight, gnawing on hot dogs and laughing carelessly. These are bodybuilders, oiled and bronzed, their ripped shirts lashed across their chests like bungee cords. These are the homeless, weathered and stinking, curled like sleeping children at the bases of palm trees. These are the conspiracy theorists, armed with diagrams of the dollar bill and essays about the Freemasons photocopied onto bright yellow paper. These are tourists, pale and ecstatic, pointing at the boardwalk populace as if they were statues.

Some days, Birdie can convince herself that it is a victory simply to be here to see all of this, a world so variegated, so different from the one that used to be hers. She can watch a woman sculpted from sand collapse into the sidewalk and feel no particular kinship with her. She can drink frozen lemonade or sit on the beach with the breeze on her face. This is not Hollywood, so she can forget, some days, the reason she came here. She can forget what she wagered.

Other days she cannot. On those days, the pieces of driftwood lodged along the shore appear to be half-buried bones. The shrieks of playing children seem full of terror. The distant Ferris wheel slowly turns, a gear that will open the creaking earth. She leaves the boardwalk trembling and the world seems full of signs. The shuttered windows of the motel rooms she passes flutter like dreaming eyes. A plane crosses overhead, circling out over the ocean and then turning back toward the east, and she can feel it pulling her with it, back to the beginning, because there is nothing here to keep her, no there is nothing keeping her anywhere.

17

Max Mason greets Birdie with two quick kisses that land in the air near her ears and then he leads her down the hallway of Serious Pictures. He pauses at a glass-walled office and taps against the glass. The dark-haired woman sitting inside looks up at him, nodding as she speaks into the headset of her phone. The rubber plants behind her desk are huddled around her like advisers. They sit in shiny black pots, their leaves thick and glossy and green, nodding silently in the draft from the ceiling's air-conditioning vent. The woman seems planted too, rooted somewhere beneath the dark surface of the desk and the leather chair where she sits, swaying slightly. Her head is in her hands, a heavy flower. She rolls her eyes and looks at her watch. Then she holds her index finger like a gun to her temple and pulls the trigger—Pow! she mouths—as she continues her conversation.

Max laughs and continues down the hallway. "Juliette Miller," he says. "Such a fucking rock star, right?"

"Definitely," says Birdie, nodding vigorously. She does not know Juliette Miller either directly or even by reputation, but it seems important to Max for her to agree with him and so she does. They need illusions of consensus, boys like this. Yes, she knows him already, the way she knows any guy in a polo shirt who walks across a conference room as if it were the green of a lacrosse field. As he walks ahead of her now— no, as he lopes—she notes his easy glances into other people's offices, the nod of his head above the gentle posture of his shoulders, his tanned neck golden against the soft white of his shirt collar—these things belong to the kind of boys who are used to people running to keep up with them, who summer elsewhere, who have cars they love and girls they don't, boys for whom not much has ever gone wrong. It is strange to think of Lewis now but she does. She is thinking that all that has happened in his life at least saved him from being this: a person she hates immediately for no good reason.

The conference room looks out into a large, loftlike space that forms the atrium for Serious Pictures' office and the dozen or so other production offices housed here. The interior atrium walls are warehouselike, lined with unpainted corrugated metal. Large black crystal chandeliers gently sway along the beam-braced ceiling. In another glass-walled room across the way, a handful of people huddle around a long wooden table pointing at the headshots scattered across its surface.

Birdie glances around the room as she sits in one of the dozen or so plywood Eames chairs that surround the conference table. "This is a nice space," she says. "Unusual."

"Well that's a nice way to put it," says Max, closing the door. "I think they call it Hollywood Danish Regency Modern. Or something." He shrugs and takes a seat. "I'm sure it was appropriately expensive, but I'd prefer to spend money on movies, not throw pillows. It's all a bit much, don't you think?"

"Well," says Birdie, aware that the entire conversation is a kind of test. "It's a statement, that's for sure."

Max smiles. On the table, a few wedges of cheese lie sweating on a plastic tray beside the skeleton of a bunch of grapes. "You want something?" he says, suddenly, indicating the remnants. "I'm sure we have coffee too." He glances back toward the closed door as if expecting to see a waiter.

She declines with a smile and they sit in silence for a moment as Max looks at her. Slowly he shifts forward in his chair. "Wow, you do have a resemblance to Melena, something in the posture. And here," he says, reaching toward her and running his finger along the side of her face. "Your jawline. Not identical by any stretch. But distinctly reminiscent." He cocks his head and squints, maneuvering her chin gently from side to side as if judging a head of livestock until finally he pulls away.

"That's what they say," says Birdie, putting her hand to her cheek as if she could feel the similarity.

"So tell me about what you've been up to," he says, leaning back in his chair.

"Well, I'm sure they told you I doubled for Melena in *The Evening Dawn*. Lighting throughout and also on-camera for nudity."

"Oh, yes, the ass shot!" says Max, nodding vigorously. He smiles. "Sorry, did that sound too enthusiastic? I saw a little of the rough cut. I know one of the editors. Dave Ender. You know him? Anyway, I hope you don't mind my saying so but . . . it's perfect." He holds the air in front of him between his palms, until he realizes he is indicating two invisible handfuls of ass. Then he shakes his head and laughs and drops his hands into his lap.

"Ha, yes. Well, thanks." Her reply is followed by a silence in which she knows they are both considering her body and of what use it may be to each of them. Finally she says, "You must be really excited. I mean, I haven't seen the script, but I saw the piece in *Variety*. Everyone's saying good things."

"Yes, yes," he says, blinking slowly. "You know, it's that same old story, the whole redneck-with-a-dream thing. But people love that story. And we're gonna make it fresh, you know? Different."

"That sounds great." She nods gravely. "People do love that story."

• • •

When Max asks, she lets him take a few digital snapshots of her sitting there in the chair and also standing in front of the corrugated metal wall. She looks up into the lens and provides smiles of varying degrees, some sweet, some sexy, some closed-lipped, some showing her teeth. Chin down, eyes up, tongue pressed to the roof of her mouth. Finally Max seems satisfied and he lowers the camera.

"There's a party tonight at the Monarch," he murmurs without looking at her as he fusses with the camera. "For Jules Dylan, the stylist. She's a friend. Do you know her? You should come."

"I don't think I know her," she says. "But I'll try to stop by."

"Yeah. It'll be good," he says, looking down at the camera's screen to review the photographs. "Okay. I think we're done. We got some good stuff. Great, actually. Look at this one. It's really . . . real."

He walks over to Birdie and shows her the image on the digital screen. There she stands, softly smiling, the angular metal wall falling into shadow behind her. Her striped sweater stands in sharp contrast to the soft waves of her hair and to the bow of lipstick she had carefully applied in the parking lot, in her rearview mirror. The effort she has taken with her appearance shows and she suddenly feels embarrassed. She sees a plaintive quality in her expression, one that can only be called desperation. *Like a redneck with a dream*, she thinks.

18

When she tells Redmond how it went, he laughs.

"Oh, God. He thinks you're *real*," he says. Then he tells her to go to the Monarch party and show her face to Max. He tells her to keep it up, the *real* thing, whatever that means.

19

There was another director, Leo King, who thought she was real too. He told her so, more than once.

I get why I dig you. You're so fucking authentic, he had said. It was the silliest line she had ever heard, an occupational hazard. He was directing her in a little part in a made-for-TV movie. Silly lines came with the territory.

The script was shit. Birdie played the college roommate of a cheerleader turned meth-head. *Sell it*, Leo commanded from the shadow beneath his baseball cap.

"Amber," she said, choking. "You just aren't yourself anymore. I miss the old Amber. We all do." And down rolled the tears.

The shoot was over soon enough. Still, it was hard to stop saying silly things as if she meant them. Leo kept calling and she kept answering. He kept showing up hungry and so she fed him. She fed him lies, one at a time, like cherries—the car accident that killed her family being her most notable invention, and there were other, smaller lies—but he liked the way they tasted, he gobbled them whole. *I'm happy*, she would say, but she wasn't happy. *This feels good*, she would say, but it didn't feel good. *Whatever you want*, she would say, but it wasn't about what he wanted. She had given up too much to care about what anyone else wanted.

When she told him about the car accident, Leo had said, *What an amazing story*. She liked the lie too. It gave her a place to put her family. They could stay inside the lie, safely dead, safely outside of discussion or explanation. She had even described their funeral: organs and flowers and shiny white coffins and a choir singing "Abide with Me." *It's unbelievable*, he said, holding her. *How strong you are.*

The lie made smaller all that was lost. The past was a shadow box and she was Gulliver, giant above it. She peeled away the walls, she lifted the roof, and she peered down into its tiny rooms. Everything was so small, too fragile for her to hold without destroying, and so she looked without touching at the tiny roads, the tiny houses, the tiny rooms, the tiny fluttering lives. Dad and Judah, driving in a tiny car to a tiny, distant place, a place in need of God; Mother, tiny in her flannel nightgown, sleeping with the velvet mask over her eyes—Birdie could hold them all in the palm of her hand. Her childhood bedroom was still lavender, a wallpaper flocked with the tiniest flowers. This was her bed, small as a matchbox. This was where she used to dream, and dreams are the only things that came with her.

Anyway, Leo eventually left. *It's complicated*, he said, but it wasn't complicated. Leo King had a wife he had forgotten to mention, a forgiving soul who hadn't cared where he had been as long as he came home. After it was over, she had called Birdie's house.

"This is Leo King's wife," she said.

"Who?"

"You know who," she said. "You're disgusting. He has a family."

"I didn't know," said Birdie, as she stood in the middle of her living room. "It's over, anyway. How dare you call me?"

"He doesn't love you," she said, crying.

"Fine," Birdie said. "If you want the truth, I don't even like him."

Leo had called later to apologize. "Don't be angry," he said. But she wasn't angry, really. In fact she began to laugh. It was the first thing that had made sense in a long time.

"Why are you laughing?" Leo asked, his voice going flat.

"I don't know," she said. "It just all seems so perfect."

20

It was the Monarch—the neon lights turning its white façade a sickly green color, the spiky plants crouching along the sidewalk, the poolside cabanas like small ivory circus tents edged with brown stripes, the green leather wing chairs arranged in jaunty clusters, the low brown daybeds piled high with linen pillows, the glowing glass lanterns defining the pool, the cocktail tables blooming up from the ground like mushrooms, the dance floor a sea of upturned faces, the music trembling over every closed eyelid, the lamps hidden in the trees bathing the party in golden light—it was the party at the Monarch that made her call Lewis.

First, she did as Redmond told her. She showed her face to Max Mason, who smiled when he saw her and came over to say hello. Palm trees loomed above them, their leaves black and ragged.

"I meant to ask you," he said. "Is that an accent? From where do you hail, ma'am?" He pumped his elbows back and forth in a little jig.

"Oh, God," she said, clapping her hand to her mouth. "Virginia. I thought I'd lost it."

"Well, isn't that lucky? It's charming. It's barely there, I promise." He squinted and blinked very slowly, indicating deep thought. "Do you know Sumner Ramsey? He's from Virginia. He did that doc about that avalanche? I think the title was *Avalanche!* You know, with an exclamation point. For *emphasis!*" He bowed his head, ready to receive her laugh.

She laughed. "I don't think so."

"Or Laura Greene? The production designer? She's working on *Where I'm From*."

She yelled over the music, clutching her drink. "No. God, sorry! I need to get out more. Honestly, I don't know anybody."

He grinned. "Well, that's not true. You know me. And you'll meet Jules, of course. Our intrepid hostess. Speak of the devil and the devil *will* appear." He glanced around. "Aha! See? There she is."

He gestured toward a woman emerging from the dance floor, blond curls sprung out in a frizzy halo, jabbing her glass into the air, splashing her drink down her wrist. She licked the booze from her arm and grinned, revealing wine-stained incisors. Her neck was draped with a thick gold chain anchored at either end by a large bronze horse head and an ivory horn. The horse nuzzled her braless breasts as if sugar cubes were hidden there, a motion which threatened to remove her strapless dress; its flimsy silk fabric was printed with the silhouettes of machine guns and fluttered upward with every movement. When Jules saw Max, she screamed with outstretched arms in a vaguely British accent: "Come here muthafuckahhhh!!!"

According to Max, they went to boarding school together. He rose to his feet and grabbed her, lifting her off the ground. Jules screamed and threw her head back and laughed, then kissed his lips greedily and beat his chest with her fists. As she watched them together Birdie felt emptied out suddenly, as if their happiness were made possible by something they were siphoning invisibly from her.

She smiled anyway. She grinned, even. She laughed along with them and had a few drinks and danced with the newly bilingual grandson of a deposed Latin American dictator and did a few lines of his Colombian in the dusky recesses of Jules Dylan's cabana. Max kept mentioning trips he had taken to

Mexican cities, overpronouncing their names: Guadalajara, Tijuana, Puerto Vallarta. *So fucking beautiful*, Jules kept saying and the dictator's grandson repeated after her, trying out the words. *Sofa king beautiful*, he chanted. *Sofa king beautiful*.

Time surged forward. They were losing moments but no one cared. They were only moments. Birdie laughed and told a story that she might have invented about a scuffle with a cop over a parking ticket. "No way!" someone screamed. She nodded violently, believing herself.

Then that feeling was ebbing out of her, leaking like air from her body. She lay back on the daybed, clutched a pillow in her arms, and listened to the roar of the party. The pillow was cool, covered with thickly woven linen and stuffed with down feathers that trembled from the music's vibrations. The fabric reminded her of something, of what she wasn't sure, but the feel of it against her face was comforting, its surface as familiar as something from long ago, something that had survived. She was afraid suddenly that whatever Max saw in her, whatever was *real*, had been lost somehow, dropped like a set of car keys and kicked to the corner of the dance floor where it lay in the darkness, waiting to be reclaimed. The linen was *real*, the trembling feathers *real*, and so she clung to the pillow, wanting to be restored. "Linen," she said slowly, pressing her face against the fabric. She imagined the pillow filling with helium, rising and taking her with it, right up out of the party.

The dictator's grandson nodded, grinning. "Linen," he repeated. Then he rose from his chair, deciding to dance again. "Li-nen!" he shouted, striking the air with his fist. He rushed out of the cabana and onto the dance floor, shouting, "Li-nen li-nen li-nen!"

"Motherfucker would've been king!" Jules shouted. "Or president or whatever. Whatever the fuck they have there."

Max's head sagged into his shoulders, concealing his neck, as if his body were slightly underinflated. "Shit," he said, gripping Jules's knee. "I could be president."

"Of like Bolivia or whatever? Fuck yeah, you could. Wear one of those little fucking hats. Ride a fucking donkey or whatever. Get some wives." She glanced at Birdie through a fringe of false eyelashes. "Right?"

Birdie searched her mind, afraid that whatever she said now might matter more than anything she had said at Serious. "Gold bullion," she said finally, filling the silence. The words hung in the air, sparkling. Birdie looked at Max to gauge his expression but he had turned to Jules, his eyelids at half-mast. He grinned and pawed at the machine guns printed on her dress. "Gold bullion. Fuck yeah. Chicks and riches."

"Perfect," Jules said. "Keep that shit in a suitcase, handcuffed to your wrist. Wear a little fucking poncho with those fucking rainbow stripes. You'd be, like, the fucking pimp." She unwound the chain from her neck and placed it on a cocktail table and then leaned back on the pillow beside Max. "You'd be flawless," she said, pushing his hair from his forehead. She slid her tongue into his mouth and pressed her palm against his chest. Max sighed and collapsed backward, pulling her against him.

Then they were oblivious, Max and Jules, buried under a pile—an *Avalanche!*—of pillows, slowing, suddenly languid, running their hands over each other. The dictator's grandson, the Crown Prince of Remedial Dancing, churned around the dance floor with his head thrown back, pummeling the air with his fists. He was sweating profusely, sandwiched between two girls in baby doll dresses and gladiator sandals and white plastic aviators. They were stone-faced and swaying, their profiles turned away from him as he ground systematically against their hips. The girls stared into space or perhaps the swimming pool, the lights from the party reflecting in the flat black

lenses of their sunglasses. They were as sober as gods, surveying the chaos of their unattended creation.

Birdie viewed this scene again through the heavy crystal bottom of her empty highball glass, held to her eye like a
monocle. The edges of everything were blurry and distorted.
Finally her gaze fell upon the horse head from Jules's neck-
lace, laid on its side on the cocktail table. She pulled the glass
from her eye and the world fell back into focus. The horse
stared straight ahead, regarding her with wide bronze eyes.
He looked put-upon, tired, and wise. He was real once too, or
an image of something that was, made of flesh and eating
oats in a barn somewhere, his head still attached to his body.
If the horse could speak he would tell her to leave. *Before they
take your body,* he would say, his lips curling to show his
teeth. *Before they cast your head in bronze.*

She stood. No one seemed to see her. "Thank you," she
said to everyone but to no one in particular.

21

It is hard to explain, but because of the horse head and the linen pillow and the cocaine and the dictator's grandson and Max and Jules and the gold fucking bullion and the lingering feeling that the party she just left would always be ending but would never actually be over, Birdie is relieved to see human handwriting, actual old-fashioned *handwriting*, on a piece of paper jammed between her front door and the doorframe. *I came by* is all it says, and it is signed *Lewis*.

Birdie examines it, considering the kind of person who, in an age of technology, leaves a note. A psycho or a hopeless romantic or someone who hit your parked car in front of witnesses, those are the choices. Lewis has the handwriting of a child or a serial killer—she is not sure which is worse. The best art department in the business couldn't do better than this. The note is crinkled and tinged with blue at its edges, as if the paper had spent some time in a pocket. The letters sprawl across the page of notebook paper, sloping and irregular, disregarding the rule. The *i* in *Lewis* is dotted with a star.

She touches the star with her finger. She allows herself to remember him: his body beside hers, the too-small suit discarded, his easy answers, his monologue of losses. Lewis was *real*. How young he was, afraid of forgetting the tragedies that made him. He did not yet know that he will never forget, that he will want to forget but will not be able. The Power-Seller mother followed him here too, grinning and selling, and the Lotus-driving father followed him here, grinning and selling, and the truth of the matter simply hasn't occurred to Lewis yet, that in order to escape anything he too must grin and sell, out there beyond the edges of what he used to be. He does not yet know that he will be compromised, just as she was. She had wanted to be true. He does not yet know that even the fabric softener commercial required compromises.

She thinks of herself at the party, the laugh, high and terrible, shrieking out of her body like the voice of a separate spirit. Her throat is raw now from that laughter, and yet in retrospect she can't remember one funny thing. She is tired of unearned laughter, of unearned everything, the lack of correlation between effort and reward. A note, this actual note, took effort. She runs her fingers over the page, feeling earned.

She stands up quickly and paces an invisible line, toe to heel, across her living room. It seems important to establish that she is sober, and she is, nearly, though the floor seems to curve slightly upward under her feet, and the sound of her step echoes too loudly off the empty white walls, and she is afraid suddenly of how fragile everything feels, as if she were pacing the interior of an eggshell.

She places the call. Her ears still buzz from the loudness of the party and the phone's ring sounds like water being sucked down a drain. When Lewis says hello she stops pacing and looks up at the wall in front of her and touches its flat white surface. It is a comfort somehow, knowing that he was altered forever long before she met him. Whatever is wrong with him is not her fault.

He doesn't sound angry, so she decides not to say she is sorry. There is effort in this, too, in pretending that the past has not happened. She smiles—*Smiles, you can hear them,* Redmond always tells her—and says, "Lewis. You have very bad handwriting."

22

There is an accident ahead. The lane of cars stretches and wriggles, metallic vertebrae in an endless spine. She will be late for her audition; another commercial she won't likely get.

Sun flashes in her eyes. She squints. She smiles. Here is Lewis, a memory from the previous night:

Seriously, Birdie said, her hand against his bare chest. *Twenty-one?*

Yes! I swear it.

I don't believe you. Let me see your driver's license.

Yes, Officer, he said. He leaned over and rummaged around on the floor until he produced his wallet from the pocket of his suit jacket. He took out his license and handed it to her.

She held it up to the light of her bedside lamp and was relieved to see it was true. Oh, well, there would be no felony tonight. He couldn't rent a car but he could drink and go to war. It would have to be enough.

See? he said, studying her expression. You should trust me.

Hugo? she said, laughing. *Lewis* Hugo *Smith?*

Okay, give it, he said. He reached for the license, but she pulled it back and held it close to her chest.

No, she said. She rolled over onto her belly, covering it with her body. The pillow muffled her voice. *I want to keep it*, she said. *As evidence.*

Lewis put his arms around her and pulled her over, moving her easily. She struggled to hide her hands behind her back. He leaned over her as if he were repairing something, pinning her down. She thrashed beneath him, thrilled by panic that seemed neither real nor imagined. She screamed high girlish shrieks that tripped and fell into laughter. He pried her fingers apart, one by one, until he had it. *No*, she gasped. *Give it back to me! Lewis! Hugo! Smith!* She panted his name into his ear. They lay on their backs, sighing and breathless. They laughed. There was no talk of death. It was perfect.

Red lights flash in her rearview. The mirror writing, A-M-B-U-L-A-N-C-E, is decoded like a secret message. She rolls slowly forward, pulling to the right to let it ease past. Through the rear windows of the ambulance, she can see the silhouette of a medic stooped over an empty gurney. He is waiting. Soon there will be a body. She pictures a moment of rescue: a body pried from a tangle of metal and shards of jagged glass, the seconds of uncertainty elapsing, elastic, the slack eyelids suddenly blinking at the sun's brightness— *Alive!* someone shouts—and finally a gasp of air taken as if it were the first, as if everything had ended and could begin again.

Before the exit to La Cienega she passes the crash. She cranes to see it but the rescue is hidden behind a high canvas barrier. She sees feet moving quickly beneath it, a good sign, she tells herself, a sign that something can be done. These things are often worse than they look; the crushed glass like rock salt sparkling across the asphalt might mean nothing but whiplash. Hope is not lost.

She grips the wheel and inches forward, staring at the car directly in front of her. She is imagining a thick white collar wrapped around a stiff neck. If the head stays still and if the eyes face forward, everything will mend. Look straight ahead and all will be right again.

23

The casting director sighs.

"No, not Wonder Woman. Wonder Woman is copyrighted. Just a *generic* superhero woman. Who is sexy. And wears a white leotard."

"No lasso?"

"No lasso."

"I feel like I should be holding something."

"You are. The tampons."

"Oh, right. Just one?"

"No, the whole box. In your left hand."

She will meet Lewis later, maybe. In fantasy, two people who have lost things could join powers to create a kind of superhero. They could read thoughts. They could leap feelings in a single bound.

24

They sit in the darkness of the movie theater, rows of people rustling around them. Lewis grabs her hand. She looks down at their tangled fingers. *Twenty-one. Ridiculous.*

The movie begins. Here, in the flickering darkness, is a moment where two lovers stand in the snow, snowflakes sticking to their hair and eyelashes, a moment of love turning sour, but no one knows that yet. The camera circles around them, dizzy with their beauty. Someone says something softly, a promise.

The story lopes through dimly lit rooms, mussed beds, blue-lit embraces, open-windowed car trips, open-mouthed laughter, until the end begins: a face glimpsed on a passing bus, the basement lightbulb, melting snow turning dirt to mud, laundry hanging on the line, only to find the backyard gate flapping open, the headlights turning away, the body asleep in the bedroom. Here is the ticking clock, the barking dog, the bad dream, here is the slow-motion running through wet grasses, the crying, the misunderstanding, here is the witty comeback, the duplicitous kiss, and the end, as it always is, a road leading into the unseen distance, implying both hope and hopelessness.

They stagger bleary-eyed from the theater. The night is littered with light pouring out of the lobby, falling down from the streetlamps, staring out from the headlights of cars as they cut around corners. Everyone is murmuring. They stand in tungsten-lit clumps assessing and reassessing the movie or finishing their popcorn or making plans for later.

Birdie waits for her cue. She is thinking of the shots they need to finish the night: cut to his arm around me, cut to the parking deck, cut to the two of us driving in silence, passing the pier, stopping at stoplights. Cut to us saying something we will or won't remember later.

He will say (the glow from the bedside lamp illuminating his face): *What did you think of the movie?*

She will say (as she stares up at the ceiling, watching the fan slowly turn): *Do you want the truth? I wanted a different ending.* (Where she knew who lived and who died, who was sorry and who was unrepentant, who would be punished and who would be forgiven, an ending that felt like an ending.)

Then they improvise. Music plays, far away. Dim light falls across their faces, revealing beauty but obscuring complexity. It is easy to believe that this is good, that this is for the best. (But in a movie, the camera would move past their bodies, to reveal first the closed door and then that sliver of light beneath it. Oldest trick in the book: the audience cannot help but wonder what is on the other side.)

25

Lewis says if the acting thing doesn't work out then his backup plan is to be a screenwriter. *It's all about stories*, he says. Birdie tells him that's like trying to be a rock star and having a backup plan to be poet laureate. Lewis agrees, misunderstanding. *Yeah*, he says. *It's all about a verse that sticks in your head*.

Anyway, he has an idea for a screenplay just in case, a movie called *The Ninth Life* in which people are like cats and have nine lives. The movie would be about a woman on her last life who misspent the other ones and so she tries to get them back. She doesn't have the heart to tell him: there is nothing science fiction about that.

26

Birdie sits on her patio, painting her fingernails and spying across the yard into the main house. The producer and his wife have returned from wherever they were and have purchased a new light fixture, a paper lantern that looks like a beehive, which they have suspended above the dining room table. The light it emits is amber-colored and even. Birdie envies this instinct to decorate. How instantly they gratify, these little improvements.

On the plastic patio table beside her, the phone begins to ring. She keeps the phone close to her, but still, she hesitates to answer. Finally she reaches for it. *Inevitable*, she repeats to herself as she picks it up. *Inevitable*. It is Redmond. "I haven't heard a peep on *Where I'm From*," he says. "Or the tampon commercial, for that matter."

"Translate," says Birdie, cradling the phone against her shoulder.

"It just means no one's talking, not today."

"I screwed it all up," she says, replacing the cap on the bottle of nail polish. "I don't know what I did. I don't know what I didn't." She holds her hands in front of her and spreads her fingers, scanning each nail for imperfections. "I did or didn't do something."

A gnat has lodged itself in the wet polish on her left index finger. She watches it struggle for a moment before finally succumbing and then she carefully removes its carcass with the point of an orange stick and wipes it off on the grass beside her chair. She hopes for a moment that she is not this small to anyone. She does not want to be removed with an orange stick and wiped on a blade of grass. Not by the tampon people, not by Max Mason.

"Remember when you didn't even want these jobs?" says Redmond. "What happened?"

That nail will have to be painted again. It will take even longer for her nails to dry now, time that she will have to sit still. Oh, well, she has nowhere to be. She holds her hands under her mouth and blows gently on her fingertips. "What else is there?" she says.

27

Now the phone is Lewis, wondering if she wants company. She is unsure of her answer, of what would be easiest. Lewis is better than most diversions because he doesn't seem bad for her, at least not in the way that drinking is bad for her or married directors are bad for her. Still, he is dangerous. He thinks he should understand everything, including her. As if understanding someone was the same as repairing them. That is the difference between them; his desire to connect the dots, to spin straw into gold, to find her bright side and then sit there shining it.

"No," she says. On the far side of her patio, a planter full of amaranth seems to be succumbing to the cigarette butts Lewis keeps stubbing out in its soil. Its red leaves are turning brown and withering. "I should be alone, I think."

"What are you doing?"

"Well, I painted my nails. And now I am watching my neighbor have a better life than me. I'm booked solid."

"Come on."

"Lewis, honestly. I'm no fun, not until I hear something. I am a vortex of negativity into which you will disappear."

Lewis hesitates, clearing his throat. "Did I tell you I had an audition too? I went to this showcase for agents. I think I choked. I was doing my monologue and they made me take off my jacket and roll up my sleeves because I was supposed to be a mechanic. I caught them . . . they were looking at my arms. The scars. Or maybe they weren't. But I thought that they were."

She drops her head to her knees. "Why are you telling me this?"

"I don't know. I thought it would make you feel better."

"You did?" She groans, lifting her head. "Lewis, please. Let's not commiserate."

He is silent for a moment. "What am I doing wrong?" he says.

She doesn't know what should come next. She has always gotten what she didn't really want, men who found her interesting because she did not speak. She did not ask them to repair the present or the past. She did not talk about the future or ask them to be in it. She told them stories that they sensed were lies or she told them nothing at all. She did not seem to want them so they pursued her to discover the reason. She was the instrument they used to measure themselves, and so they crouched beside her, they fumbled as they held her body and they searched her expression for clues. There they saw what the camera saw, a certain detachment that they could fill with whatever they wanted, and maybe Lewis was the sweetest, the youngest, the most naïve of these men, but still he was one of them. He searched her for what he had not yet found within himself, hidden depths of love and complexity. He had not yet guessed that she was empty. She might tell him this if it weren't for his scars. The scars are horrible but also the best part; they reassure her that his optimism has limits.

"You're not doing anything wrong," she says finally. "It's me."

"Let me take you somewhere," he says.

Birdie sighs. Her neighbor, the producer's wife, has arrived home with her arms full of errands. She places a grocery bag on the kitchen counter and disappears into a hallway with a sheaf of dry cleaning covered in plastic. How normal, Birdie thinks—buying groceries and light fixtures, tidying things, making a life work—all of it seems so simple, and yet it's like watching a gymnast. Back flips only look easy.

Birdie stares at the glowing beehive, all of that lovely light. She says, "Where will you take me?"

28

One of her former acting teachers, the singularly named Otto—a name he had given himself because he thought palindromes were lucky—once required everyone in her class to switch living spaces for a day, to see how interacting with someone else's environment might change them. Her partner in this exercise was a comedian named Billy Lex. She spent the day watching cartoons and pornographic movies in his Culver City rental, a dark studio apartment decorated with vertical blinds, an air mattress, piles of dirty clothes (his *floordrobe* he had called it), an orange nylon life vest, an oar, a water bong, two acoustic guitars with broken strings, and a selection of dorm room posters: Escher's stairs, a kitten hanging from a tree branch, a jazz trumpet entwined with a single rose. Perched on top of the television was a silver-framed photograph of Billy standing next to a woman whose face he had obliterated with black marker—all that was left of her was her neck and her dress.

When the day was over, Birdie returned home to find Billy Lex smoking a joint on her patio and staring across the yard. When he saw that she was home he shook his head and pointed toward the main house and said, *That.* Then he stood up and walked over to her. *You gotta get out of here*, he said. *Everything's so . . . close. But far. You know?* She told him that he was right, that she knew what he meant, and that it was only a matter of time. He asked her what she thought of his *pad* and she said, *It made me sad. It's a sad pad.* Billy nodded and said, *But you were sad when you got there. Weren't you?*

He took her face in his hands and shook his head. *Everything's sad when you're sad*, he said. She nodded and closed her eyes and hoped that he wouldn't remember this later, this letting him tell her what she was, this letting him cover her with stoned, dopey kisses, this letting him know that he understood.

Now she watches the sun set in Runyon Canyon with Lewis's arms around her, aware that he is something she will regret later, listening to his dreams. In this one he was clinging to the spire of a tall building, blasted by the Santa Ana winds, until he finally lost his grip.

He says, "You know that feeling, that falling-in-a-dream feeling?"

"Yes," she says, watching his lips. They are reason enough to regret something later.

"It's such a surprise to wake up, isn't it?"

"Yes." She nods and looks away from him.

Then for a little while there is silence and for that she is grateful. They look out into the failing light. They could see all the way to the ocean from here if it were not for the smog hanging thick and gray as cobwebs along the horizon. When the Santa Anas come in, the smog will get pushed out to sea and the air will get hot and dry and wild and if you can keep from flying off the edge of something, you can see for miles.

29

"Two things," says Redmond, the voice that wakes her.

"Two?" Birdie says, arranging the phone against her face. "What do you mean?"

"God, were you asleep?"

"No," she says. She pulls herself up into a sitting position on the couch.

"It's, what? Noon. That's my girl. That's healthy."

"Redmond, you have two things? Tell me." Across from her couch is a window that looks out onto the alley. Birdie stares outside, head thick, willing the details of the days into focus—bicycle, lawn sprinkler, red truck, barking dog. Lewis left late, she remembers that.

"Grab a pen and paper. You'll want to remember this when you emerge from your blackout."

She reaches into her purse and pulls out a pen and grabs a magazine subscription card from the coffee table to use as paper. "I'm ready. Tell me."

"Okay, write down the following: Dear Diary, Something good happened to me today, and it didn't involve lubricant and a minor."

"Fuck, Redmond."

"Exactly." He laughs. "Okay, two things, Birdie. Two good things. One, you got a callback for the commercial. This Wednesday."

"The tampon thing? You're kidding me. I was terrible."

"Well, whatever you did, do it again, because they liked it."

"Oh, God, I don't want to be in a *tampon commercial*. How awful."

"Residuals, chickie. Suck it up."

"Yeah, yeah. Tell me two is better."

"Two is pretty fucking good," says Redmond. His voice is calm. "I heard from Serious."

"And?"

"Well, here's the thing. They're not doing a double for Melena. They don't have the cash for it. You know how it is. Indie budgets, they've got to cut something."

"And I'm happy about this?"

Birds are calling to each other. There is a distant horn blast. And then Redmond says these round, perfect words like pearls sliding onto a string, making everything suddenly lovely, complete. "Max wants you . . . to audition . . . for the part . . . of Melena's . . . sister."

30

Nobody understands Crystal Bishop, not her mother and not her father and especially not her sister, that bitch Libby Bishop. Nobody appreciates duty anymore or the toll that it takes, nobody sees that Crystal, that faded flower, that bitter blossom, that angel of the meatpacking plant, is a girl who wants what is best for her family, who leans forward to accept the yoke that they place around her neck even as her heart screams to escape it, even as she dreams of leaving the aprons and the carcasses and the practical shoes far behind her, of pulling a carpe diem and getting the hell out of there goddammit! Of course, she stays. Crystal would have done well scrubbing an Elizabethan chamber pot, perhaps. Her morality is a relic.

Nobody sees the anger and regret that boil inside Crystal, especially not Libby Bishop, that savvy goddess, who flitted off to New York City or Miami or Chicago (TBD, pending location scout and cooperation from local city government) and who landed a glamorous job as a restaurant publicist with just her wits and joie de vivre. No, sushi-eating, Riesling-drinking, lawyer-dating Libby had no trouble leaving behind the burdens of her mother's illness and her family's poverty. How could she be so selfish . . . and yet so enviably full of life? One must think that such a girl contains vast reserves of feeling and compassion deep down inside, reserves that will most certainly be discovered when the going gets tough, when she returns to *Where* she is *From* in compliance with her mother's deathbed wish. One must assume that she has a good heart.

"So basically I'm the ugly one," says Birdie.

"Not *ugly*," says Redmond. "A little tired."

31

"Super-extra-mega-dry! Super-extra-mega-dry! Super-extra-ultra . . . shit." Birdie flips the script over and looks at it. "*Ultra-extra-mega. Ultra-extra-mega. Ultra-extra-mega.*"

Lewis is lying on the patio, staring up at her. "Well, you can sell the hell out of a feminine hygiene product," he says. He starts to laugh. "God, I hope you get it."

"Yeah, you and my checking account." She opens her fingers and lets the page float to the ground beside her chair. Then she picks up the *Where I'm From* script and walks over to Lewis. She gazes down at him. Sprawled out on that slab of cement, in his dark suit and sunglasses, he looks like a fallen secret agent. Only he is grinning. She nudges his body with her bare foot. "Now come on," she says. "Help me with the real one."

"You don't get to come back. I don't want you to." She turns her back to him.

"But," says Lewis from somewhere behind her.

"But nothing. We're doing just fine without you, after not being fine for a long time."

"I needed to get far far away from here. I was bored out of my mind. There was nothing for me here."

"There's nothing for you here now, either," she says, turning to face him. "So you might as well leave." She starts to cry.

Lewis stares at her in silence for a moment, his cigarette

dangling from his mouth. Then he remembers the script. *"I'm sorry,"* he says. "That's as simple as I can make it."

Her jaw tightens. "No, sorry isn't simple. Leaving is simple. So go on and do it again." She pushes past him, crying angrily.

Then Birdie sighs. She walks back across the patio, wiping her eyes. Her palms are wet and she wipes them on the lapel of Lewis's jacket. Then she puts on her sunglasses and picks up her drink and takes a sip. "Am I even close?" she says, looking at him.

Lewis nods and runs his fingers down the length of her ponytail. "Ultra-extra-mega-close," he says.

32

In the darkness of her bedroom Lewis says he's never seen her cry before and Birdie says that it wasn't her crying it was Crystal Bishop and he asks if she is sure because she was awfully convincing. She turns toward him. She says that she is certain.

33

The ad agency people keep glancing at each other. The director sighs. He takes off his eyeglasses and wipes the lenses with his shirttail.

"No, *ultra*-extra-mega. *Ultra*-extra-mega," he says.

"What was I saying?"

"Super-mega-ultra."

"Oh sorry. No super."

"Yeah, scratch the super. And ultra comes first." He slides the glasses back onto his face and his eyes reappear.

"Right."

"And don't drop extra."

"Extra." She nods. "Got it."

"Now, tone. I'm thinking, overall, I could get a little less . . ." He purses his lips.

"Energy?"

"No, less . . . vibration." He holds his hand at eye level. "You're here," he says. "I need you here." He drops his hand to chest level. "Make sense?"

"Yes, yes. That's actually really helpful."

"Great. Just . . . keep it real, keep it quick." He pops his fist into his open palm. "Like that," he says. "Boom."

"Got it. Definitely no problem," she says.

"Good. Let's go again," says the director. A guy at the far end of the client couch, someone from the agency, is passing a note to him, grinning a shitty grin.

As she smiles and looks back at the camera, she hears the note unfolding.

34

In the parking lot it is Birdie Baker, not Crystal Bishop, wearing a white leotard, vinyl car seat hot against her thighs, who cries.

35

Another dream. Birdie opens her eyes to yellow newspapers and faded wallpaper, red clay and rusted swing sets, dusty bookcases and calling voices. No, this is Venice and the sun isn't up yet. The body beside her is Lewis. She curls into him, violently.

"What is it?" he murmurs.

"Tell them to leave," she says into his chest.

"Who?" he says, stirring.

Those voices belong to people passing on the street. Sleep opens beneath her, soft and deep. "Nobody," she says, squeezing her eyes shut, holding on to him, falling into it.

36

The day of the audition, Redmond drives Birdie to Serious. As they cross through the city they pass car washes, taco stands, tire rehabilitators, clothing boutiques, fast food joints, nail salons, donut shops, furniture stores—storefront after storefront, each some combination of cinder block, stucco, and plastic. Persian rugs and chandeliers and shoes and sweaters crowd against their windows. Banners advertise grand openings and imminent closings along with varying degrees of discount, and unfurled on the sidewalks, leading up to the shops, are rubber utility mats made to look like red carpets. Light flares up across the glass façades of buildings and the metal bodies of cars as they drive. As they approach Sunset, Birdie savors glimpses of the hills beyond it. She thinks of how, from that distance, this chaos is transformed into something twinkling and lovely and benign. Height, yes, elevation is what she needs, the narrow road that leads up to where it is peaceful, among the fragrant trees. Down here, chaos sprawls in every direction, the concrete overpasses darkening the streets that crouch beneath them, the hulking frames of billboards standing like sentries along the freeways, the flat expanse of faces staring out from them, lovely and immobile. Below them, the populace of the city; tucking quarters into parking meters, milling on sidewalks and street corners, carrying shopping bags, chatting on cell phones, squinting behind their sunglasses, cleaning their windshields as they fill their cars with gasoline, running squeegees over those vast fields of glass in broad and careful rows like farmers plowing land.

Birdie does not understand what satisfaction any of it can bring, to be, as they are, camped along the base of the mountain, always looking up at the houses perched like temples above them, imagining their gilded interiors, the wealth and splendor of the ones who inhabit them, the certainty of their minds and the deep peace of their sleep. It does not seem possible to live without searching oneself for a way up, for beauty or birthright, faith or delusion, talent or luck. From here to there is the distance between what she is and what she could be. She has seen herself from that distance. She has looked down from those very hills and has seen how very small she is, so small that she is indistinguishable from the rest of this mess, too small to see and, should she disappear, too small to miss.

"Don't be nervous," says Redmond.

"I'm not." Birdie looks up into the vanity mirror. As with any lie, she will say it until she herself believes it.

"You should be," he says. "So I can tell you not to be. That's my job. To make you feel better."

"Well, I am now," she says, surveying her eyes, her mouth. It is what it is, this face. She can't change it, not in the space of a car ride. She flips the vanity mirror shut.

"Good," he says, glancing at her. "Don't be."

37

Leo King once let Birdie watch casting tapes with him in his hotel room, auditions for the part of a girl with multiple personalities in his next TV movie. The meth movie had wrapped a few weeks earlier and Birdie lay beside him on the bed, drinking coffee from the room service tray and watching all of the pretty girls introduce themselves to the camera: Olivia, Alice, Kelly, Anna. Leo would view each girl for a few moments and then skip past them. He tore bites from buttered pieces of toast as he mumbled at the television screen: "Boring. Boring. Bad skin. Boring. Old. Boring. Bimbo. Boring." The girls blipped by, their smiles jump-cutting from one to the next. They were smiling at the chance they thought they had.

Birdie looked at the toast crusts accumulating on Leo's plate, a pile edged with his teeth marks, those jagged, greedy bites. "How rotten can you get," she said, rubbing his neck. "You should watch their whole audition."

"I want someone to wow me," Leo said, pulverizing the toast in his mouth. He skipped ahead again, staring at the television and chewing rapidly, taking quick, squirrel-like bites, his unshaven cheeks enlarging as they filled with bread. A fine mist of crumbs fell down into his open shirt collar and disappeared into the dark curls of his chest hair. Finally, he took a swig of water and swallowed.

She dug her fingers into his shoulders. "Leo," she said. "Those are people!"

Leo shrugged her off and smiled, his lips slick with butter. "Yeah," he said. "They are people who aren't getting this part."

Later that night in that big white bed when she asked Leo if she had wowed him in her first audition there was such silence she could hear the ocean heaving outside the window. How beautiful that room was, with the fireplace burning in the corner and the hurricane lamps filled with seashells perched upon the mantel, the hardwood floors reflecting the fire, the air smelling of salt and burning cedar, the bright white duvet and the bank of down pillows, and a row of shutters wide open to the ocean, ushering in the calls of gulls and evening breezes. The night could have been perfect. But when Leo said "Of course," he said it without looking at her, and so Birdie took his face between her palms and looked into his eyes and said, "No, really. Tell me." Then he grabbed her breasts in his hands and moved down her body, kissing her softly, so he did not know that she was crying when he whispered, "You're wowing me now, trust me."

38

Handshakes and nice-to-meet-yous. They tick off their names: Danni Berman, Juliette Miller, Linda Wise, Barry Wall, Joe Cameron, Max Mason. They stand and sit down again in a fluid wave, like baseball fans at a game. Max says how happy he is to see her. "Everyone is," he says, whispering in her ear as he kisses her cheek.

"Let's get started," Linda says. "Why don't you stand right here, so that Joe can get a nice shot of that face? I'll read with you, as Libby."

Birdie and Linda stand at the end of the conference table, its surface studded with scripts and bottles of water. At the back of the room, Joe turns on the video camera; its red Record light blinks for a moment and then turns solid.

"Give us a slate," says Linda. Joe nods, his eye to the camera.

Birdie looks at the lens. A casting director once told her to *be ginger ale* when they slate you, effervescent and golden, sparkling and sweet. *Make them want to drink you*, he said. And so, always, when she is slated, she cannot help but picture a mouth closing around her. She says her name and smiles gently at the camera. Chin down, eyes up, she turns to both sides, giving them her profiles. *Swallow me*, she thinks.

"Got it," says Joe.

"Great," says Linda. "I guess we're ready then."

"Action," Max says, from his seat beside the conference table.

"You don't get to come back. I don't want you to," says Birdie.

Linda searches through her glasses for the words. "But," she says.

"But nothing. We're doing just fine without you, after not being fine for a long time." She folds her arms in front of her chest.

"I needed to get far far away from here. I was bored out of my mind. There was nothing for me here." Linda makes a small gesture with her hand, indicating the conference table.

"There's nothing for you here now, either," says Birdie. "So you might as well leave." Her voice cracks on the word *leave* and then she begins to cry.

"I'm sorry," Linda says, shrugging her shoulders and shaking her head. "That's as simple as I can make it."

She pushes the tears away with the heels of her hands. "No, sorry isn't simple. Leaving is simple. So go on. Do it again." She tightens her jaw and shoves past Linda, into the dead end of the corner of the room. She stands there facing the wall, waiting for Max to call it.

"Okay!" says Max, leaping out of his seat. "Cut cut cut." Birdie turns around and smiles and places her script on the table. The room is silent for a moment and then Max begins to clap and nod vigorously. A smattering of applause follows.

Redmond leans in to hand Birdie a tissue. "Mascara," he whispers. She looks at him, dabbing her eyes until he nods.

"Beautiful," says Max. He nods vigorously and turns to Juliette Miller. "Beautiful, right?" he says.

"Yes," says Juliette, smoothing with her hand the script that sits closed in her lap. "Really, really lovely."

39

Redmond maneuvers the car around the crowded parking lot and through the front gate. They sit in silence at the end of the driveway and wait for a stop in the flow of oncoming cars. Birdie stares out her window at a palm tree withering by a bus stop, its trunk black with exhaust, its fronds brown crepe paper streamers that flutter briefly when a bus passes and then hang limp again.

"Well, you were fantastic," says Redmond finally. "Max loves you, clearly. And Juliette Miller. She calls the shots and she was positive. Cards held to her chest but that's her reputation."

"*Lovely?* Tea parties are *lovely*. Weddings. And the way she said it . . . like it was a euphemism for *absolute shit*."

"Lovely is great," says Redmond, glancing at her. "Lovely is beauty with a dimension of grace."

"Redmond. Crystal Bishop works at a meatpacking plant. If I was *lovely*, I got it wrong."

"Hey. If white trash couldn't be lovely I would've told you to go home a long time ago."

"It's interesting that you think that's a compliment." Birdie stares through the windshield at the empty street. "You can go now," she says, waving her hand. "There's nothin' comin'," she drawls.

"I wouldn't make jokes if I didn't think you'd nailed it," Redmond says, touching her shoulder. "Come on, chickie. Look at me."

She looks at Redmond, leaning her head back against the

headrest. She wonders if, behind his sunglasses, his eyes are tender. They might be. He runs his thumb over her cheek, wiping away a remnant of something. "Look at this," he whispers, holding out his thumb to show her the wet black smudge. "Actual tears. Call the anthropologists."

She leans in, pretending to look. Then she grabs his thumb between her teeth. His thumb is salty and thick and she bites down hard enough to leave a mark. She smiles.

"Nice," says Redmond, pulling his hand away and examining the two half-moons of teeth marks imprinted along his thumb. "You are biting the hand that feeds you. Literally."

"You said it's your job to make me feel better. And now I do." She leans her head against his shoulder and sighs. "I do feel better."

Redmond makes a little noise that sounds kind of like a laugh and pulls forward into the street. She looks up at him, considering his profile. "What?" he says. "I see the wheels turning."

"I'm still seeing him. He's really sweet." She is only dimly aware of why she invokes Lewis now: to remind Redmond to believe in her. Whatever else may happen, she can incite desire.

He responds without looking at her. "And yet here you are. Biting other men's thumbs."

Birdie's smile slowly fades. She pulls away from Redmond and rests her head against the glass of the passenger window and they sit in silence watching the same scenery they passed on their way over: the same crappy car washes, the same crappy parking meters, the same crappy everything. "Does Carine know anyone at Serious?" she says finally.

"Of course she does." Redmond shrugs, his eyes still on the road. "And *if* I see her, I'll ask what she's heard. Carine's found herself a script reader. Fresh out of college. He's *fun*." He throws his hands up in mock exasperation and then grips the steering wheel again. "It's an epidemic. Fill me in on the appeal, would you? Is it the premature ejaculations? The acne? The Japanese cars?"

"Redmond."

He doesn't look at her. "Let me guess. He *holds* you for *hours*. I could hold you for hours. Not *you* literally. But let's talk capabilities . . . if he's giving two hours, I could go three. Two and change, at least, unless my arm falls asleep. There's the young buck's advantage. Better circulation."

"Um, yeah. Circulation."

"Don't talk to me about your sex life." He shivers. "But yes. The flow of blood. To the extremities." He glances at her. "You know it's not Carine, right? It's the losing. I mean, Carine is this *socialite* who acts like a *maid*. She likes to *fold towels*. She likes to *replenish* things." He makes a swirling motion with his right hand, indicating her zone of influence.

She stares out at the line of traffic in front of them. "Why would you take La Brea?"

"Because I hate us both and I want this to last forever." He sighs. "She can't let anything just *be*. So, I get it. Mommy wuvs baby. Baby wuvs mommy. She'll clean his room and make him . . . applesauce. Mash it right up."

She nods. The traffic advances and they roll slowly forward.

"Don't nod at me. What's your excuse?" He glances over at her. "You're no socialite."

"So, what? I'm . . . poor and lazy?"

"I'm saying . . . you're not making applesauce. I don't know what you're doing with that kid but you ain't making applesauce."

"I wasn't aware that I needed an excuse," she says. "He's cute. We run lines. We . . . improvise."

"*Of course* you do." Redmond grins and stops at a light. Two nannies pulling red wagons full of toddlers cross the street in front of them. The expressions on the children's faces range from fear to ecstasy. One kid sleeps, slumped over like a drunk. "Never mind. I love a girl who improvises. A girl who . . . bites." He makes a show of examining his thumb, holding it close to his face and squinting at it. "A little redness, but nothing permanent." He kisses it. "There, there," he whispers. "She didn't mean to hurt you. She never does."

They sit in silence for a while, watching the world through the windshield. At a corner a few blocks later, Birdie notices a woman standing at a pay phone. A Carl's Jr. star hangs smiling above her. She is holding the receiver to her ear and shaking her head violently. Her ponytail whips back and forth. Her roots are gray but the ponytail is a harsh black, as if it had been dip-dyed. Birdie thinks of calling home, just to hear those hellos. "Redmond," she says suddenly. "How was I? Really."

Redmond glances over at her, registering her expression. "You killed it." He takes a deep breath through his nostrils and nods, agreeing with himself. "I think you could get it. Believe me?"

The woman at the pay phone is holding her hands to her face. Her shoulders heave up and down. Something is lost, something is over, or something is gone.

"Tell me you believe me." Redmond takes Birdie's chin in his hand and turns her face toward him. In moments like these, sometimes she has the urge to close her eyes and lean forward just to see what would happen. She isn't sure she wants to know. So she keeps her eyes open. The lenses of Redmond's sunglasses are impossibly black, but she can make out the edge of his eyelashes. *How reliant you are on a gaze*, he once told her, and his is somehow reassuring, the blink of his eyelids as steady as a metronome. She wants to believe him. He called the county and dug up the details. He put her to bed and gave her a peach-colored pill and a drink of water. He is the man in the armchair, the voice of reason, the hand that feeds her. His mouth is grave, his forehead is sweating slightly, and in his upper lip she detects the littlest twitch, as if he were about to bite her back. He reminds her of a tent preacher ready to heal, with coiled snakes hissing in his pockets.

She shivers. Praise be. "I believe you," she says, and a bus groans past them.

40

Lewis isn't where she left him, lying in a shaft of sunlight on her unmade bed. The shaft of sunlight isn't there anymore either. Lewis is temping at a law firm, where he stamps incoming mail with its date of receipt and then places it in one of fifty-eight in-boxes. The shaft of sunlight has moved over the roof and onto the patio, where it filters pink through Birdie's closed eyelids.

Lovely. She weighs the word in her mind, feeling its slightness slip away from her like a scrap of paper lifting up into a draft. She has an urge she immediately suppresses, to call Leo King. Leo had been good at this sort of thing, dismantling flattery into its cruelest, truest meanings. *Quirky* meant *bizarre*, *sweet* meant *inconsequential*, *maternal* meant *unfuckable*.

On their trip to Mexico, when a maître d' at the hotel restaurant called her pretty, Leo corrected him. *Beautiful*, he said. The maître d' capitulated quickly, nodding and bowing deeply. He brought them flan later, *con cumplidos*. So that was Leo. *Pretty* never meant *beautiful*. The hotel was on a hilltop (the hotel was pretty, the hilltop beautiful) with views of the sea and carved wooden parrots on the walls and bath towels the housekeepers shaped into swans each morning. They ate ceviche with saltines that came in little cellophane packets and drank cold white wine out of green glass tumblers. One night they lay in bed and watched a lizard crawl across the ceiling.

There was a moment on the beach—Leo walking ahead

of her, shirtless, in corduroy shorts, with a blue towel flung like a scarf around his neck and large, ridiculous sunglasses he had purchased at the airport—when the space between them seemed to expand, like the tide shrinking away, exposing a black stretch of sand. At a great distance, she saw suddenly a man who thought she was *beautiful* and *real*, a man who had kissed the sole of her foot when she cut it on a broken seashell and who, when she recounted the fictitious demise of her family, had tried to comfort her. He was the *real* one. *How strong you are*, he had told her. But she wasn't strong. She was only pretending. A row of pelicans flew single file over the water and she released the thought, not knowing what to do with it.

There was no need to solve it. They were both pretending, after all. Six months later in Santa Barbara, Leo told her *it's complicated*. She stared past him, at the repeating pattern of sea grass embossed on the restaurant's foil wallpaper. *Yes*, she said, nodding. She looked for the seam where the pattern repeated, and when she found it, she looked back at Leo and smiled, relieved that she did not love him. *It's complicated* meant *it's over*, something Leo didn't need to decode for her.

41

She needs to leave the house. She walks up to the boardwalk and stops at a pay phone on one of the low concrete shacks that house water fountains and public restrooms. It is low tide—something that always disconcerts her—the ocean dragging away from the shore. For a moment, she considers how miraculous it is for her to dial these few numbers and have a phone ring three thousand miles away. As with the tide, this process is invisible and beyond her comprehension. She closes her eyes as the line begins to ring. The scene comes too easily: the mustard phone on the cornflower wall, the sticky kitchen table, the rings echoing off the busted linoleum. No one answers. She pictures the hallway, swallowing any sound into the silence of its carpet and its swaddling of newspapers. Birdie redials the number but again there is only ringing.

She disconnects the line and hangs the receiver back in its cradle. She considers the explanation for her parents' absence only briefly. The answers that come quickly—church services or errands—seem likely and sufficient.

It is getting late. She retrieves her coins and takes a seat on the low stone wall that divides the ocean walk from the beach. Soon it will be sunset and already the exodus has begun. Pink-skinned tourists dizzy from the sun stumble toward the parking lots carting bright red coolers. Their tubes of aloe, their modest bathing suits and cargo shorts, their performance fabrics and preponderance of pockets, their new hats, their pale feet, so exposed and vulnerable . . . she is thinking of her parents still. For a moment Birdie imagines a series of scenarios, all of which release her mother and father from their bunker and deliver them blinking, mole-like, into the actual world. These scenes flash by as small and bright as postcards: a house at the beach, every wall a window, with a deck where they could nap and read newspapers; a trip to the desert, where they could ride burros into canyons and take photographs of sunsets; a cruise, where they could watch for whales on the starboard deck and eat at the captain's table. It is like wishing Buckingham Palace for them, along with the monarchy of England. None of it would happen. Even at the beach, they would sit at the kitchen table and watch the ticking clock. They would remain inside their safehouse until all that was nigh actually arrived and the walls collapsed around them, revealing Paradise.

Breezes fill the air with the smell of incense, a heady mix of sage and patchouli and knockoff fragrances, making her feel suddenly claustrophobic. A pair of teenagers lie on the beach in front of her, their limbs and hair tangled together like seaweed. Sand clings to their skin in a thin sparkling layer, as if their bodies had been molded from this very beach and then given the breath of life. They kiss languidly. They touch each other's faces, amazed. Birdie watches them openly, as if they were on television. She is too old for this. She is no sand nymph, no teenager. But she longs for Lewis, the white noise of sex muffling the world into silence.

Birdie rises and begins the walk home. A rollerblader swoops past her on the concrete footpath. He seems to welcome the obstacle of the bodies he passes, carving a neat arc around each of them as if they were all statues. She stands frozen for a moment with the breeze on her face and everyone rushing past her.

She is thinking of endings. The best ones are biblical.

There is the story of Lot's wife. When she looked back with longing at the doomed city, God turned her into a pillar of salt. As a child Birdie had found the story terrifying and therefore compelling. One of her earliest remembered dreams was of a vast wilderness full of frozen people, like the statues in her grandmother's courtyard, their salt-white bodies turned to face a burning city. In the dream she wandered among the statues, uncomprehending. Wind howled over the hilltops. She had looked at the city, she had been filled with longing, and yet she had remained unpunished. But it didn't feel like forgiveness. Those flat white eyes looked past her, longing for all that was lost.

These aren't dreams, these women passing on the boardwalk, their faces frozen into expressions of serenity. They are photocopies of their former selves, too white, flaring out into blankness, the contrasts softened, the edges lost, the accuracy forgotten. Former actress. Former model. Former. She can distinguish them easily. They walk slowly. They hold their beauty upright like a vase full of dying flowers. They hold it with a death grip.

That night, Lewis is not a person. He is Time, rolling back above her. He is a clumsy god, unaware of his power. Clouds race backward, turning dark and then light and then dark again. He breathes into her, pulling her from the sand. Heaven, that cloudless atrium. They should be marble. They should be like this forever.

42

They didn't decide to go to anywhere. They just went. You turn onto roads and follow them. The roads do the rest. The Pacific Coast Highway to Malibu, leaving the Ferris wheel behind you. There, everything faces west: the guardrails, the stacks of houses, the lifeguard stands, the silhouettes straddling surfboards out beyond the break. Sometimes Birdie forgets that it is Lewis driving beside her, the feeling of being a passenger so familiar to her, of being steered through the world by wills other than her own.

Then down again, to the winding stretch of Sunset. From the Palisades to Echo Park the city reimagines itself—the manicured junipers, the pathways of palm trees, the gold and stone buildings, the canvas tents, the hidden hotels, the temporary locations, the lingerie stores, the fitness centers, the neon ranches, the pole dancers, the place where it happened, the chalk on the sidewalk, the comedy clubs, the billboards, the Thai massage, the liquor store, the dance studio, the burger joint, the high school, the record store, the empire, the painted wall, the junction, the reservoir—until you're in the parking lot of a taco stand and you don't remember how you got there.

They sit at a picnic bench, Lewis exhaling smoke from his cigarette into the already gray air, the wrappers from their lunch on the table in front of them. He squints through his own cloud of smoke, his tie still flung over his shoulder to avoid any spills. "It's pretty awful," he says.

"Why don't you think of it as a scene?" she says. "That way

it's not as bad. Like you are not *actually* a temp at a law office. You're just *playing* a temp at a law office. Like an acting exercise."

He considers this. "Okay. So then yesterday I had a scene where I put mail into everyone's in-boxes. And I had a scene where I ate lunch by the fountain outside and I had a scene where I got yelled at for not filling out my timecard the right way and I had a scene where I stole a notebook from the supply cabinet."

She laughs. "Yes. Exactly."

"I guess. Seems like a pretty boring movie." He gestures at the 99-cent store across the street and she turns to look at it. Its windows are crammed with boxes of detergent and pink plastic watering cans and gallons of antifreeze and tubs filled with brightly colored candy and cellophane wrappers holding stacks of paper napkins. A woman stands by the storefront, her arms laden with plastic bags. She squints at the horizon, silent and sweating. "So that woman waiting for the bus should be thinking, *I'm just playing someone waiting for a bus. This is the scene where I buy a bunch of crap at the 99-cent store and wait in the sun for a bus that won't come.*"

She turns to face him. "Maybe."

He shrugs. "Look at that place. We should be in the plastic and candy business."

"I thought we were." She smiles.

He seems not to have heard her. He is still gazing at the 99-cent store. "Yeah. Maybe it's better to think that none of this is really happening. I mean, who really wants to be in there? Buying a bunch of stuff that's gonna break on the bus ride home? You're right. You can't think about it that way. You have to think: this is just one scene. And who knows what the next one brings?" He touches her hand, hearing himself. "I guess I'm just sick of it. The being poor part, I mean.

Being nobody." He stubs out his cigarette. "Temping . . . my starring role."

"*The Temp*," she says, making a frame in the air with her fingers. She looks at his face through it. "Yes, yes. The face, the lips. The eyes. The *intensity*. I would buy a ticket." She drops her hands to the table. "Okay. Come clean. How many scenes with the hot young legal secretary?"

He rolls his eyes. "She is a stereotype. Bad casting."

"I knew it! She exists." She looks at her hands. "You can do what you want, Lewis. I mean, we haven't made any promises. You should be . . . I don't know."

"Drinking Jäger out of a sorority girl's belly button?" He closes his eyes, feigning contemplation. Then he nods. "Yeah, that's exactly what I want. You just solved it for me."

"I just mean, being young. If you want to be. I don't know. Forget it."

"I'm kind of done with the young thing." He says this without looking at her. He squints out across the parking lot, as if his youth were a coin he had dropped, a flash of silver he might spot on the sidewalk.

"Lewis. I didn't mean it. I don't know what I meant." But he has forgotten her for a moment, his eyes focused still on some small and distant spot—a glinting coin, a receding point, a thing to remember. She grabs his wrists and tugs him toward her. Finally he looks at her. "I'm not *actually* an asshole. I'm just *playing* an asshole," she says. She touches his face. "Lewis. Kiss me."

He moves in stages, as if remembering choreography. He takes her chin in his hands, runs his thumbs over her cheekbones, then pulls her face to his. Sunlight flares golden through his eyelashes. This kiss is eyes first, side-lit and colorless, then breath, teeth, and lips. It is a response to accusations both real and imagined, this kiss—his tongue probing her mouth, her hair caught up in his fist, the width

of his hand on the back of her neck, the office worker soft-
ness of it—and when he pulls away from her, all has changed.
He is hers again, and for a moment she is disturbed by how
easy it was. But only for a moment. The sun settles back into
its hilltop.

They walk to the car and he holds his palm steady against
the small of her back. Plastic flags snap in the breeze and
their shadows stretch long and black across the gravel lot.
And once again they are kicking up dust, leaving the blocks
behind, watching for brake lights. What a mess the sky is,
the black hills stacked with layers of cloud, gray and orange
and green, like sedimentary rock, pressing down on everything.

These scenes are the stuff of montage, of memories. *That
Day in Echo Park*, she'll call this. They stop for gas and
Birdie watches through the window as Lewis lifts the nozzle.
He has removed his jacket and rolled up his shirtsleeves. He
is a silhouette and Sunset is the vanishing point behind
him, its neon weak in the twilight. He taps a rhythm on the
window with his knuckles and leans down to look at her.
Fluorescent signs flatten his features with their white-green
light. He is wearing the gas cap like a tiny hat. She laughs.
He stands in the light from the car's headlights, hooks his
thumbs into his belt loops and does a little dance. It is a pup-
pet's jig, all knees and elbows and grin. Birdie hollers and
claps. Lewis smiles and removes the hat and stretches his
arms out above him, ready to receive his applause. He bows
to an invisible audience.

43

One of Otto's exercises started with empty coffee cups, one for each of them. *Pretend they are full of liquid*, he said. They held the cups gingerly, glancing at each other, taking great empty gulps. *Careful*, he said. *It's piping hot.* And so they blew into the cups and warmed their faces above them. They took careful, tentative sips. Billy Lex dropped his cup into his lap and leapt to his feet, howling. They all laughed. *Exactly right*, Otto said. So they took turns throwing invisible drinks into each other's faces. They staggered around the studio, laughing and feigning pain.

Each week was a new incarnation of this exercise, which Otto called the Invisible Kingdom. They were passengers in an invisible train watching invisible scenery pass through invisible windows. Billy Lex was the conductor, shouting out stops and punching invisible tickets. They fixed invisible cars. They popped invisible hoods and probed invisible engines. They lived alone in invisible apartments and watched invisible televisions. They smoked invisible cigarettes and stared into invisible refrigerators. They took invisible showers. The important thing was never to pretend. *These worlds are real*, he told them. *You just have to see it.* It is amazing how much is made possible just by imagining it. Marriages, pantomimed into being. Children, sprung whole from daydreams. You build it with your mind. You forget that you are surrounded by nothing.

At the last class meeting they had an invisible dinner party. They dressed in imaginary finery and primped in front of invisible mirrors. They lit invisible candles, passed invisible platters back and forth, and chewed invisible bites of meat until their jaws grew tired. They picked invisible pieces of gristle and bone from their mouths with their fingers. They poured brimming glasses of invisible wine, cut large pieces of invisible cake, and ate every last invisible bite. They licked their fingers and loosened their waistbands. Someone rose to put an invisible record on an invisible phonograph and Birdie leaned back in her chair to listen. She watched invisible candlelight flicker on the walls. She swayed to silent music, satisfied.

44

Two weeks of the phone not ringing. The days went this way. Birdie lay on the bed until the sunlight left and then she followed it out to the patio. The idea was, if she followed the sunlight, if she kept it above her, she was not a person lying in bed in the dark.

In the afternoon she would leave the house in need of something. There would be no more glances backward, no calls home, no pay phones. She would walk along the sidewalk, her eyes focused on whatever was in front of her. She would buy cups of coffee or magazines, give tourists directions, pet other people's dogs. She lived in a world of minor transactions, a stream of pleasantries that somehow verified her existence. She lingered at the folding tables along the ocean walk listening to the rants of radicals. She accepted flyers. She entertained the causes of others. She decided they were right about the Freemasons. She agreed about marijuana. She thought she might be a feminist. These conversions passed through her like spirits, possessing her temporarily and then, as each medium moved on, abandoning her body.

Home again, she would lay crumpled receipts and flyers and cocktail napkins across the kitchen table, whatever she had gathered during the course of her day. They were crucial, these bits of evidence. They reminded her of jigsaw puzzles, how you lay out the pieces to make sure nothing is missing. Then you group by color and parse the details. You wait for the picture to emerge.

Here is a picture: a cup of green tea, a copy of *Vanity Fair*, a Free Tibet flyer, a thin leather bracelet purchased from a Rastafarian, and a still-cold cocktail shaker. Here is a life she could've lived if she had thought to live it. She could've spent some time on a houseboat, maybe bummed around Southeast Asia. She could've meditated and gotten some cheap massages and worn some saffron-colored robes and come back to LA with glowing skin and a clear head and an armful of prayer rugs and pottery. She could've learned how to paint patterns in henna on the backs of people's hands. She could've moved to Portland, Oregon. She would be there now, in a house full of teak furniture that she bought at yard sales and flea markets. She would be mostly vegetarian but have a steak each year on her birthday. She would vote Democrat, but be a member of the Green Party. She would drive one of those old Mercedes that run on French-fry grease and she would read Anaïs Nin and drink lychee martinis and have an aloe plant in her bathroom. She would keep chunks of cut cantaloupe in a Tupperware container in her refrigerator and have Tantric sex with the owner of a Vespa repair shop. They would call it lovemaking. When they got tired she would feed him pieces of melon from the plastic container and he would lick the juice from her fingers and grin and then kiss her slowly, his mouth still cold from the fruit. She would close her eyes as he covered her body with cold kisses. She would fall back on the bed and let it all begin again, listening to the sound of wind chimes ringing outside her window, because in that life it is easy to begin again and in that life she would have wind chimes.

Byron Everett used to give her shit for this when she was a student in his private workshop. *Imagining a life is easy*, he once told her. *Living it is the hard part*. In preparation for an audition she once filled a dozen pages of legal paper with a character's motivations—her medical and sexual histories, the layout and furnishings of her apartment, the contents of her refrigerator and handbag, the make and model of her car, her hobbies, her fantasies—and then she showed the whole thing to Byron. He read the pages, slowly and almost sadly, before finally looking up at her. "Or you could *feel* something," he told her.

There are calls from Redmond, none of them news from Serious. She did not get the tampon thing. The hooker murder thing is happening—Rex Peters has signed on to star—but they are retooling the script. In light of the other (Maggie Mayo) hooker murder movie in production they are taking another angle on the material; the story will be sci-fi, set in outer space. There might still be a role to try for, ostensibly some kind of space hooker, but nothing is confirmed. Redmond invites her to lunch once or twice, the equivalent of a mercy fuck, but she declines. She would not be able to help turning the conversation into a discussion of her deficiencies, the only topic that seems currently available to her. It is an ugly compulsion, but in her mind a sensible one. She wants to fix herself, that's all. If she knew what was wrong she could fix it.

Lewis orbits her life at a constant, elliptical distance. She is relieved when he arrives and relieved when he leaves. She is afraid that she needs him. No, she is afraid of the space that he occupies and its emptiness without him. She is afraid of her own mind, the gray playroom for her terrors. They shuffle toward her across the floor. Their teeth glint in the twilight.

When she is thinking of Lewis she is not thinking of Max Mason and what *real* means to him. She is not thinking of Leo King or whether she *wowed* him. She is not thinking of the difference between *lovely* and *beautiful*. She is not thinking of the ringing phone or the halls stacked with newspapers. She is not thinking of poison air or the sound of

Judah's footsteps in the hallway. She is not thinking of the cliché she is becoming. It is like handing a toy to a screaming child. When Lewis arrives she is quieted.

Sometimes he calls from the law firm and describes his day to her, the scenes in the hallway and the copy room and the mailroom and the library. How he improvises with difficult costars. How predictable their dialogue is, just the kinds of things that people always say to each other. No, none of it seems real anymore. But the place looks so perfect, just like a law firm should look when you picture it: the heavy wooden desks, the old-fashioned lamps of brass and green glass, the dark suits and dark shoes, the blue dress shirts with white collars, the outdoor plaza where he eats his lunch, the fountain shooting jets of water into the air in a series of pulsing arcs, the firm handshakes, the power ties, the closed-door meetings, the wine-colored walls reflected in the chair railings, each room so hushed and quantifiable.

She does picture it. She lies in bed with the phone pressed to her face and wills this world to form around her. She sees Lewis in his shrunken suit, dreaming past the file folders. She smells aftershave and hears the low hum of computers. She walks down carpeted corridors and stands in doorways and watches a shaft of sunlight move across the mahogany tables. She waits in silence. She causes no disturbance.

45

Signs, everywhere, in no particular order.

In the newspaper, Birdie reads reports of a tidal wave someplace far away. Photographs of before and after. Before: roads and huts and people and cars and carts. After: a riot of mud and bodies, brown water and broken things. *We thought it was the End,* a villager said.

Also a 5.4 hit in Chino Hills, big enough to feel in Vegas and San Diego. A girl in a Silver Lake coffee shop saw what she called crop circles in her latte. *And I was like, whoa,* she said, holding out a trembling hand.

Lewis leaves a message after seeing a billboard for *The Evening Dawn* somewhere on the 405. "Her head is on *your* body. That's you up there and nobody knows it!" He sighs. "I'm sorry. I guess I just wanted to tell you I knew it was you. And the part that was you was beautiful." The message is like a shot of novocaine, delivering a bright stab of pain and then a dull, lingering numbness.

She makes and remakes her bed again and again. She unplugs her alarm clock. She barely sleeps and when she does she dreams of a house that is vast and continuous, an endless series of rooms and stairs that leads always back into itself, like the Escher poster on Billy Lex's wall. In the endless house she can go up or she can go down but she can never get out. She closes her bedroom door and goes down the stairs and opens the door and her bed lies dark and rumpled in front of her. Billy Lex sometimes appears, sitting up in the bed with pillow creases on his face. "We should leave," he says and then goes back to sleep. God is also in the dream. He has no face, like the girl in Billy's photograph. He hovers above everything, a vast presence, like the house, never-ending and infinite.

The neighbors' lights go on and off at unprogrammed times. Sometimes they play music that leaks through the windows. Sometimes their laughter leaks too. Birdie lies on the couch, drowning it out. She watches television, mostly cooking shows, hour after hour of women planning parties, preheating ovens, feeding children, chopping garlic. They assure her that none of this is complicated.

She will section a lime. She will make a gin and tonic. Gin and tonics are different from scotch—they are cheerful, they make her think of summer. In the grocery store, she cannot find a perfect lime. Each one seems to be decaying, studded with brown spots, scars, or malformations. She asks the boy in the produce department, "Why is everything rotten?" She feels her voice getting high and strange. He shrugs his shoulders and pushes his mop across the floor.

Finally, she buys the juice that comes presqueezed in a lime-shaped plastic bottle. Back at home, she squeezes the juice into her drink, forming a stormy little lime-flavored cloud. She stirs it and brings the glass to her lips. Yes, this is it. Finally, something perfect.

46

Before and after. Later, Birdie will describe the change as a color, the world shifting from gray to silver, a gleam that builds as the earth turns toward the sun, leaving night behind for morning. There was no sound of trumpets but she remembers a squawking teapot like the call of seagulls in the morning as they swoop over the still green canals.

Before. The tangled gray days, the depthless nights, the pale walls and distracted kisses, the shifting freeways, the worry creeping like vines over her body. That morning: the teapot simmering on the stove, the ringing phone, the run to answer, the hesitation, the volition, the surrender to admit the inevitable—the news on the other end of the line— and then hearing Redmond's voice, as familiar as pain.

"Pack," he said, simple as that. "You got it, chickie."

"Really?" she said, trembling. The teapot began to whimper.

"Yes," he said, as resonant and certain as God.

After. Birdie floats through rooms turned suddenly silver. The teapot screams. She picks it up. "There, there," she says as it moans and goes silent. Her pulse throbs softly in her neck. Suddenly there is comfort in her. She sips tea and then rinses the cup and dries it and places it back in the cabinet. She waters a plant on the patio, wanting to take care of something. She leaves a message for Lewis. *Good news*, she says. She can do all of this, easily.

Then she walks up to the boardwalk, anxious for contact with the living world to disprove her suspicion that all of this is only a dream. Bodies pour past her like sand. A breeze shifts and moves along her face. Voices and laughter lift into the air like kites. The Ferris wheel slowly turns, as benign as the hills behind it. The world washes over her like water and subsides, catching along the length of her body without taking her with it. Like driftwood, she remains.

She looks with benevolence at the clamoring people, the roiling ocean, and the yellow smog looming low over all of them. Suddenly she is full of pity and forgiveness for Los Angeles and the earth and also God. They were not lies, those stories—about the Ones who mopped floors and washed dishes as they waited for the Rapture that would carry them upward and who were at last plucked from steno pools and chorus lines and lunch counters, rescued from obscurity like refugees ascending the rope ladders of Red Cross helicopters. All that came before was a lesson, the scheme that got her here, to a moment where the earth seems to slow and turn silver and she is certain of her place upon it. She is *Birdie Baker, Actress*. Finally, the future.

47

Anybody who is anybody has stayed at The Mount Maraca. Some people live here for a while, when an indiscretion is publicized or while a house gets remodeled. Some people die here, on expensive sheets in reclining poses, with pills left scattered like candy across the nightstand. There are rumors of ghosts in the hallways. And there are parties, of course. The hotel is so frequently a scene of celebration that the parties often feel like reenactments of each other, each new occasion a facsimile of the last, with a beautiful girl in a sparkling dress, just as there always is, screaming with laughter and draining her glass, just as she always does.

Years ago, in a moment of optimism, Birdie decided The Mount Maraca would be the setting for her celebration, the place to toast The Part when she got it. She had been to a friend of a friend's New Year's party in one of the airy suites upstairs, a drunken snowstorm that left her lost, wandering along the corridors and tripping over the carpets. She darted down the hallways with outstretched arms, dragging her fingers along the walls, remembering something: running in long grasses under the deep blue of a darkening sky. She was looking for ghosts. The flocked-velvet wallpaper felt alive against her fingers. When she looked up she expected to see bats swooping in the twilight but there was only music up there, above the ceiling. She followed it. The next day she awoke on a blood-red carpet in a room littered with bottles and bodies and plate after plate of uneaten cake in heaps like Roman ruins. She looked down at the sleeping people sprawled across the floor and realized that one of them was a famous actor. And so she stayed for a little while longer, eating fingerfuls of frosting as she watched him sleep. She touched his famous lips with a sticky finger, leaving a shine of sugar there. His eyelids fluttered just inches away from her as he dreamed. Everything was so wonderful, she wondered what was left for him to dream.

So here is a suite. Here are two bottles of champagne and two plates full of cake. Here is music. Breezes from the gardens outside drift through the open window, carrying with them the smells of the hills that loom just above Sunset, of lily and eucalyptus and gardenia.

Here is Lewis, woefully miscast for a scene of celebration, his body draped across the bed like a Roman ruin. Birdie hopes he is finished saying how happy he is for her. It is clear that Lewis's store of happiness is finite. By spending it on her he has less left for himself. Each time he says how happy he is for her he seems to vanish for a moment, as if he is uttering a spell that erases everything except a smile, not his smile, but a smile he borrowed for the occasion. Like his suit, it doesn't quite fit.

She is rescued, finally, by Lewis's own piece of good news, something he was hesitant to mention at first. An agent from the showcase had called, offering to get him work as an extra. Lewis hadn't wanted to talk about it at first. *It's your night*, he kept saying. But it is exactly what they need, the weight of some good news to place on his side of the scale, to set them in balance again.

A sticking point, perhaps: the agent suggested that Lewis change his name. He thought *Lewis Smith* was too plain.

"Help me think of one," Lewis says. They are lying on top

of the bed, facing each other. His expression is his own again, the false smile returned to whatever prop trunk it came from. He runs his hand along her leg. She is wearing a very short pale blue silk dress and a very thin silver lamé coat that she couldn't bear to take off because it was just too pretty and a large pair of rhinestone earrings that catch the light and refract it into thousands of pinpoints like stars across the ceiling. She feels giddy suddenly, from the suite and the dress and the champagne and her relief that the earlier awkwardness has vanished. Now they have this new game to play.

She rolls onto her stomach and leans over Lewis, studying his face like a doctor examining a patient. She pulls his lower lip down with her thumb and looks at his teeth, squinting. "What about Jackson," she says. "Or Jude." But as she says the names, she knows they don't fit. She frowns. Jackson would be a redhead from Mississippi. Jude would be short and from Liverpool. She peers into each of his eyes. "Henry? Henry." When she says the name it doesn't sound fake. *Henry* sounds like church bells, old-fashioned but familiar. She holds his face between her hands, as if she were measuring the width of his cranium. "Yes. And you could use your middle name as your last name. *Henry Hugo*. It has a ring to it." She can picture him, Henry Hugo. He looks just like this.

He wrinkles his face for a minute but then nods. "Okay."

She pushes his hair to the side of his face. "They might call you Hank."

"Yes, ma'am," he drawls.

She laughs and shivers and draws against him. "They'll only let you play cowboys. The bad ones."

"Well pick another one, then."

"No—Hank. I like black hats. You see that hat coming and you wonder: What's he gonna do?"

He laughs. "Yeah. Well, you were working at that saloon

and I came back to get you." He hooks his fingers over her hips and smiles. "Didn't I?"

It is like walking through a door that has been opened for her. She doesn't know why she walks through, only that in the hotel room there was a balance to be negotiated between them. It was all too precarious, the distribution of their happiness.

"What did you do, Hank?" She whispers the words with her palm pressed against his chest. In this new room, kerosene lanterns have replaced the table lamps and her dress is made of faded calico. The walls are slats that creak in the wind and every noise in the hallway just might be the sheriff's deputy.

He shakes his head. "That was a long time ago, honey."

"Did you kill a man, Hank?" Even the music playing on the stereo fits; the song is just dark enough to soundtrack the question.

Here is Hank's face falling sad and serious. He looks past her at a vast pile of cowboy regrets. "Whatever's happened, I'm real sorry." He touches her hair. "I'm a changed man. I promise."

She holds his face in her hands. "Hank. What's going to happen to us?" she whispers. But the question is too real, taking them back to the beginning. She does not want to say anything that applies, not tonight. They look at each other, wondering. There is not enough room for both of them, these worlds real and imagined. Lewis—no, Hank, let him be Hank—kisses her and she embraces him, pulling him toward her. She asks no more questions. They roll back on the pillows and her rhinestones throw their sparkle across the ceiling. Doves fly up from their dovecots. And in the street outside, the gallop of horses, the clatter of pistols, the howl of the train whistle, the shouts of lawmen.

48

"Let me guess," Redmond says, looking her up and down. "You're back on the market."

"No, I'm not *on the market*." She takes a seat at the table, smoothing her sundress beneath her as she sits.

"Well, that's an on-the-market dress." He folds his newspaper and tucks it under his chair. "Isn't it a little early in your career to wear sunglasses indoors?"

"It's just a dress. And it was a late night." She grins and wiggles her eyebrows above her sunglasses.

Redmond shakes his head. "You have the sex life of a repressed Midwestern businessman. On a trip to Thailand."

"Please. It's just a sex life, Redmond. It has nothing to do with the *market*."

As Redmond signals the waiter he tells her, "It has been my limited but undeniable experience that twenty-one-year-olds don't know the difference."

49

All she said to Lewis was this: *Wish me luck*. Asking for this wish from him was a bit like asking for his participation in planning his own assassination. Whatever luck he wished for her, if it had any power at all, would no doubt carry her away from him. But she wanted to be carried. They had been frozen together in a single frame of static, the Pause button pressed, and now a great finger hovered above them, contemplating her release. And she wanted to be released. She wanted all of the things that would take her away from him, but if she did not get them then she needed Lewis, the comfort of his gaze, his beauty frozen beside her in that gray and white frame.

He did, of course, wish her luck. He wished her luck and embraced her and told her there was nothing to worry about. He said it several times—*There is nothing to worry about*—and each time he said it she deflated a little, like a helium balloon descending slowly from the ceiling on the morning after a party. There was everything to worry about. All she had was a chance, and chances are only as good as the people to whom they are given. This was the chance, she was the person, and she did not know if she was good.

50

On a legal pad, she writes the following:

Crystal Bishop.

Contents of handbag: keys to car and to locker at
meatpacking plant. Keychain is plain and possibly
devotional. Jesus?? Flavored lip balm (cherry). Older cellphone
(black plastic). BIC lighter. Virginia Slims. Kleenex. Hand
sanitizer. Faux designer wallet containing: a debit card, her
high-school boyfriend's senior picture, her driver's license
(the photo is oddly flattering—in it she looks better than she
does in real life), gas card, membership card to local discount
superstore.

Car: 1991 Chevy Impala or similar, looks like it could belong
to an undercover cop. A few dings but mostly clean. Air
freshener hanging from mirror (new car smell or vanilla,
NOT PINE). Possibly devotional? I heart Jesus?? In well
between front seats is plastic Big Gulp cup that she reuses to
hold Sprite mixed with lots of ice (she chews ice when she's
nervous, which is often). Hair scrunchie on gear shift.
Change in change well is mostly pennies and sticky from
spilled Sprite.

Refrigerator: Fridge is shared with mother but there is a shelf
devoted to Crystal's special food items (a small way to assert
independence). On her shelf she keeps a 2-liter bottle of Sprite,

string cheese, crunchy peanut butter (her mother likes smooth), and dill pickles (her mother likes sweet).

Hobbies: watching TV, going to yard sales and civil war reenactments, reading People magazine, smoking (on the sly).

Sexual History: At twenty-five, still a "technical virgin." Rounded third base with her high-school boyfriend (who has since married and moved to Norfolk, VA). Was recently tongue-kissed and groped (over sweater) by married meatpacking plant manager. At the time, she didn't really want to, but she enjoys thinking of it in retrospect. Has never had an orgasm. Too shy to masturbate (God is watching).

House: shares pre-fab home with mother. The kind with plastic siding. Furniture is rent-to-own, the stain-resistant, built-like-a-brick-shithouse stuff you see in doctor's waiting rooms. Television has old-school antenna (no cable) and blue tinge to the picture. Gets mother to record soap operas on VHS tape for her when she's at work. In her bedroom: a framed needlepoint of "Footprints" given to her on her sixteenth birthday by her now deceased grandmother. A stuffed rabbit she keeps in her underwear drawer (but at night she takes it out and sleeps with it). His name is Succotash. An assortment of drugstore cosmetics are scattered on her bureau (she doesn't actually wear makeup but she has the fantasy of having an occasion to wear it, and of being the sort of person who would know how to properly apply it). On her bookshelf: the Bible and a few mystery novels featuring crimes solved by single, attractive assistant district attorneys who drive BMWs and own their own condos.

Medical History: Allergic to mold. Sneezes easily. Dry cuticles. Insomnia. Would like to ask for a sleeping-pill prescription but is afraid of becoming a sleep-eater (she saw something about this on the news).

Fantasies: Becoming a marine biologist or an assistant district attorney or a real estate agent. Owning her own condo. Being "taken" by a lumberjack or other woodsy type in a log cabin on a bearskin rug in front of a roaring fire. (Though not technically rape, as she would both want and enjoy the sex, she needs to think of it that way. The lynchpin of the fantasy is sex exempt from any personal responsibility.)

Most positive feelings about Libby: At one point in her life, Crystal felt protected by Libby. In most photographs, Libby has her arm draped around Crystal's shoulders (the bitch was always taller than her, always). Also, when Libby left she forgot to take a coat that Crystal still wears. Everyone tells her she looks good in it.

Most negative feelings about Libby: Ongoing fantasy that Libby dies in plane crash and due to a new inheritance law the contents of her bank account go directly to Crystal. Also her car and condo.

51

They want her tan for the movie. "Like you've been rolling in a dirt patch," Redmond said. So on the day before she leaves, Birdie goes up to the spray-tan place on Montana, the usual place she goes when it's required. She strips down to nothing and they stand her in the middle of the booth and close the door and turn on a mist that sprays out over her skin from hundreds of little nozzles in the walls. They always say she doesn't need to but still she holds her breath. The booth makes a sound like a vacuum that stays in her head long after she leaves.

Stopped in traffic on the drive home, she adjusts the rearview mirror so she can see her face. She watches the nuances of her cheeks, her brow, her eyes, and her mouth as she forms these words: "You don't get to come back. I don't want you to." Horns sound behind her and she rolls forward toward the setting sun. She sneers at the girl in the mirror and then she says her next line. "We're doing just fine without you, after not being fine for a long time."

The tanning spray leaves her skin golden brown and smelling like the wet sprouted eyes of potatoes. In the middle of the night she wakes up and sees the dark silhouettes of her legs and arms against the white sheets and for a moment she thinks they belong to somebody else. She does not feel connected to that body. Her heart begins to pound and she lies perfectly still. She sends a thought down into her leg and on into her foot, a thought to wiggle her big toe, and when her big toe wiggles she is relieved. This is the body she is taking back to Virginia in the morning. No, this is the body she is taking to Virginia for the very first time. There was nothing before now, nothing except this girl and her history. Crystal Bishop is three things she never was: tan and obedient and too afraid to leave the place that she came from.

She arranges the sheets to cover her body completely, up to her neck, and goes back to sleep.

52

She dreams a dream, which is also a memory.

In Virginia, for a long time they have had reenactments of Civil War battles. In humid dawns armies of firefighters and general contractors and social studies teachers dress in the blue and gray uniforms of soldiers. Their wives pack coolers. They drive to one-time battlegrounds that have been transformed into soccer fields. Then, wearing suspenders and waving flags, they line up the cannons. The sound is almost like cannon fire, the firecrackers they light. Soldiers crawl across the dirt on their bellies. They advance, unrelenting. Then, in great clouds of smoke and with panicked shouts, they begin to fall.

Birdie witnessed one such reenactment on a grade school field trip. She had found it boring. She had not understood the appeal of acting out old battles. These wars were already over. Everyone knew the ending already. There were already winners, already body counts. So she just stood there, unsurprised, waiting for it all to be over. The only detail she remembers liking was the nurses. They wore bright white uniforms. They stood under sun tents in nervous clusters, ready to pretend to save someone.

In Birdie's dream, they are filming a battle scene. She can't tell whether it's a real battle or a reenactment of one. Nobody in the dream can tell the difference either, not Max or Melena or Redmond or Lewis or Leo or Judah or her parents. Everyone is there but no one seems to see her. They are watching the battlefield, unsure of what they are witnessing.

The nurses are in the dream too. They stand around the war in a bright white circle. Ribbons of gauze dangle from their fingers. They are waiting for something terrible to happen.

53

Just a thought as the landing gear engages and the ground rushes up beneath her: it took nine years to get one hundred miles south of where she came from.

54

South Hill, Virginia. Three weeks that felt like nothing, that passed so quickly because all of the time that came before them was suspended, the white-walled room where Birdie had waited for her life to begin.

The automated wakeup call was a voice without enthusiasm. In the hazy gray dawn Birdie would stumble up the stairs of the makeup trailer into air sharp with the smell of coffee and sparkling with face powder, sometimes nodding asleep as they leaned over her, as they flattened and tangled her hair and left her features undefined. "Country face" is what they called it. Then Birdie would look up into the mirror and make peace with Crystal Bishop before stumbling back down from the trailer and out into the humid, blooming morning.

Daylight, daylight from another time, poured from the sky like syrup, like amber honey, slow and sticky, binding the days together. The locations shifted beneath her—the sagging porch of a mouse-brown house, a vacant lot studded with rusted-out trailers, a dirt yard strung with laundry lines and littered with broken toys and cinder blocks, a parked car, a courthouse, a knobby creek winding along a muddy hillside—all of these places seemed strange and lovely, changed, in that light. They seemed to be memories, as did the trees and kudzu that tangled along the way, that formed tunnels and walls along the low twisting roads that they drove, their leaves and branches breaking the daylight into fragments that scattered across Birdie's face like broken glass.

Sometimes they were ready for her and sometimes they were not. Sometimes Birdie would wait and watch in silence as the world was constructed. Frames dotted the landscape, being assembled or dismantled. Silks and scrims sagged and flapped against the grass until they were pulled tight and raised on silver stands, wide and white against the sky. Grips crossed back and forth, hauling sandbags. Max darted between the video taps, blocking shots within the slender frame of his fingers and murmuring to Soren, the French cinematographer. Then they would both stare up at the sun. Set dressers ran by with hubcaps or dinner plates or sundials in their hands. Production assistants drooped against trees and trailers, smoking cigarettes or talking on cell phones or eating bananas, waiting for direction, the mics of their walkies clipped to their collars. They stooped along the perimeter, collecting litter in the garbage bags tied to their waistbands. They had hoped for something more glamorous, it seemed, than waiting for someone to need them.

Albert Dave and Juliette Miller moved over those fields like ghosts, gripping cups of coffee and wearing black coats. Sometimes Juliette would emerge from Melena's trailer and run over to Max. She would whisper into his ear and he would shake his head and Juliette would whisper again, gesturing with her pale hands. Beneath the shadow of his baseball cap, Max would nod and shrug his shoulders, and then look at the assistant director. "Change of plan," he would say, shaking his head as Juliette walked away.

Sometimes Melena would greet Birdie as she passed, bobbing her head quickly and smiling as she walked to her trailer. Sometimes Melena pretended she didn't see her, staring through her body as if she were invisible. She would say hello instead to the grips and the production assistants with a wide smile that was meant to show she was not afraid to be contaminated by them. Once inside her trailer, curtains drawn, Melena would leave only for her scenes or to practice yoga with her hairdresser in the low grass behind the honeywagon. There she would bow down, pressing her face to her knees before rising up and saluting the sun with both hands.

One day Birdie heard the script supervisor say, "I had expected better." She knew she was referring to all of them and the chaos they had created. They would scramble, decide, and change their minds. Some days it rained and they would stand in clusters like cattle under hastily assembled canopies. Some days Birdie went through makeup and her scene never came. "You'll never guess," the AD would say, out of breath and clutching a clipboard to his chest. The local grips kept disappearing—for safety meetings, they said, a code that the line producer didn't know. "Right now?" he would ask as the sun moved across the sky. Their names blared from the radios that jutted from the hips of the production assistants sent to search for them. They would be found gathered in slope-shouldered clusters, leaning against the lift gate of the grip truck, smoking weed out of hollowed-out hammers.

Eventually it would be time for Birdie to say her lines—no, for Crystal Bishop to speak her mind—in a driveway, on a porch, or by a laundry line. Melena would stand beside her, made taller by an apple box. They would wait for silence, for the lawn mower to stop mowing or for the plane to pass overhead, and as they waited Birdie willed away the world—the sunlight and flashes of color, Max's hunched shoulders, Melena's breathing, Melena's glance, the waiting grips, tiredness, the sounds of people chewing, the drop of sweat rolling down her back, the walkie's crackle of static, the mosquito bite on her ankle, ignoring the itch, the shifting breeze, the treetops bending over, over—until her thoughts fell and scattered like dead leaves.

When silence arrived Birdie said the lines that sprang up inside her, the ones that she had remembered. This was not the past or the future, these were only words, and because she was saying them, in this moment, they were hers. Melena's eyes darted back and forth, searching her face for approval. No, this was Libby Bishop, prodigal daughter, beautiful and brave. She wanted forgiveness for running away. And here was Crystal Bishop, lovely but faded, angry and afraid. She had stayed.

"I had to," Libby said, crying. "Try to understand."

Crystal crossed her arms and shook her head. "Never," she said.

The landscape sprawled around them, green and wild, crawling with crickets and honeysuckle vines. Birdie was aware of the sun bouncing off the silver boards they had erected around her. She was aware of Max staring into the video monitors. *Let the light find her*, he would murmur. *That's it*, he would say. *Look up. Look up.* She was aware of Juliette Miller and Albert Dave, hovering after two or three takes. They were running out of everything: time, film, patience, money. Then Max would say, *Beautiful. Let's move on*. As Melena and Juliette and Albert walked away Max would tell Birdie, *We got what we needed*. She nodded at Max, burying her thoughts. She wanted assurance that she was changing something, that what they were doing had the power to transform everything that would follow, but there was no way of knowing.

Max was battling Serious about the ending. Until now, they had agreed that the finale should be not a resolution but a lull in the battle, a day of peace, brief and bittersweet. Now Serious wanted to add a scene: an apology from Libby to her family. It would make her more sympathetic, they insisted. Birdie heard Max complaining to Soren about the rewrite. "What's so good about sympathetic?" he said. Soren shook his head and shrugged. "They want everyone to be good inside," he said, a goal that sounded especially trivial in his French accent.

Sometimes they would stand in those fields and watch the sky. They were waiting for the earth to turn, waiting for the magic hour that brought with it beauty, the angle of the sun that would transform their silly cluster of kudzu-draped trailers into equal parts bleak and beautiful, a Southern Gothic landscape, green, black, and gold. The hour would always arrive promptly, just above the rooftops, and for her close-ups Max would thrust Melena into that forgiving light.

Birdie would stand and wait with all of them. She would stand in the long grasses and watch as Melena's face flickered in the monitors, as Melena pretended to know what it felt like to lose things. "Forgive me," she said, blinking. Cicadas began to buzz in the treetops, a sound like static that grew louder and louder, and as the sound grew louder, it seemed that everything was moving farther and farther away from her. It was over already even as it was happening. The world had been silver for only a moment. Now it was gold, the color of the light they saved for Melena. Melena, the camera her mirror, gazed into its depthless reaches and asked it to confirm what she already knew—that she was beautiful. There was that smile, Melena's smile. How they waited for it! They watched the monitors as people watch the sky for comets, until there it was, that streak of light across the heavens. Max and Juliette would nod in silence, the camera gobbling film until the night fell down around them. Then, in darkness, the world was dismantled. They moved back across the fields toward the yellow headlights of the production vans. Engines trembling, they moved Birdie toward a future that looked almost exactly like the past.

Redmond left a variation of the same message every day. "Do you hate her yet?" he would say. "I watched *Mind Games* again the other day. I mean, have you seen the girl's crying scene? It is like watching a poodle pull an oxcart." Then he would recite the list of things he was doing to turn this role into the next one. *Parlay*, he liked to say. He called her from the treadmill usually, and he panted the information into the phone. Her name had appeared in *Variety* and the *Hollywood Reporter* and *Entertainment Weekly* in coverage of *Where I'm From*, and so Redmond was chasing down things, opportunities. As he said these things, Birdie imagined her name in tiny letters swimming in a sea of type and headlines. He said they had a working rewrite of the Rex Peters project—*Light Year*, they were calling it—but she would have to audition again. The hooker assassin was now a murderous alien disguised in human skin. Her reasons for killing have something to do with a biological imperative. She would have seven lines and be kissed and killed by Rex. A small part but memorable, Redmond insisted, if she got it.

Lewis called and left a series of long messages. He was careful to say he expected no reply. In one message he said he was Henry Hugo calling from the set of *The Temp*. He said he just had a scene where he got fired for sleeping on the job. He hadn't meant to. After lunch out on the plaza he lay on the low concrete wall beside the fountain and watched those jets of water shoot skyward. He found it soothing, he said. That's the last thing he remembered, all of that water pulsing right above him with the sun behind it. When he opened his eyes again there was a silhouette leaning over him saying it was time to leave.

He said it would be all right. The temp agency found him a new gig at a telemarketing company that sells penny stocks, where he opens envelopes and stamps the backs of incoming checks and types names and addresses into a computer form. Most of the checks are from Florida or Arizona and are written in shaky handwriting. He described the room to her, the rented furniture and the temporary walls and the fluorescent buzz and the rows of cubicles like cattle stalls. But it would be all right, he insisted. He had decided to think of the job as a part in a boiler-room drama, where he plays the new kid, the one they underestimate and who exposes everything, how everybody is a cheat and a fake and how greed ruins everything. Shot from above, the whole thing could be classic De Palma.

In his last message, he said the agent from the showcase turned out to be a flake and never came through with any extra work. But it would be all right, Lewis said again. He has other ideas. He has an idea for a screenplay called *Seventeen Seconds*, based on his personal experience. There was a Cure album of the same name, but he was sure something could be arranged. After all, he had actually died for seventeen seconds, not sixteen or eighteen, and he assumed he owned the option to his own life story. The movie trailer would feature a silhouette standing in a field of white light. He wasn't yet sure what the plot of the movie would be exactly, but it would be something about getting another chance to get our lives right. Yes, it would be all right, Lewis said, pounding the words like a piano chord over and over to drown out the low hum of his doubt.

It was always this from Lewis, bad news delivered along with the reassurance that all would be well anyway. As if reassurances could erase what came before them. She pictured Lewis standing at the law office copy machine, his face illuminated by the light that sweeps across its glass surface, scanning the depositions, turning the pages, and gathering them into a careful stack. She pictured him hunched over his desk at the telemarketing company, opening envelopes and stamping checks, examining the handwriting, the trembling penmanship of grandparents, the naïve loops, the shaky vulnerability. She pictured him telling himself that none of this was really happening. Lewis never wanted to be angry, even when he should be. That was no way to live. She can see the anger inside herself, hard and dark and glittering, and though she doesn't trouble herself with its origins she has some dim idea that she might have been a happier person had she not been disappointed so often. But that's not what happened. She was disappointed, she was fearful, she was weak, and there are prices to pay for all of these things. Lewis has reasons for anger, same as her, same as anybody, and how he came to believe that he should be exempt from these feelings is a mystery. How hard it must be, pretending the feeling does not exist even as it grows inside him—that dark curling presence, the rage turning over, its bony hands and blind eyes and hunched shoulders. You had a brother who died, Lewis, and a drunk for a mother and a Jungian analyst and a father who replaced his sons with sports cars. You are allowed.

She sat on the edge of the bed with the phone pressed against her face, wishing she could tell him something. She wanted to tell him that it is not all right. She wanted to tell him how her body is filled with straw and how her eyes are sewn-on buttons, how stiff she is, how dry and hollow and dirt-crusted. How tired. How they prop her up in an open field. How crows fly in circles overhead. How she gets mixed up sometimes. How every night she has to cross a very narrow bridge back into her own mind. How she waits there for daylight. How in her dreams she wanders through unfamiliar rooms picking up objects, all of them made of glass: glass candles, glass flowers, glass photographs. How invisibility persists.

Instead she lay motionless on the bed. The sheets were rough and turned her skin red when she moved and so she lay still, waiting for sleep. Then the past arrived, rubbing against the window screen, and that poison air descended upon her bed. There was nothing new to remember, nothing new to feel, there was only that same accumulation of losses, but here, with the smell of honeysuckle all around, with the days spent in a green, humid haze, and with the lines she spoke still humming in her mouth, the venom of their judgments, she felt them more clearly. Absence after absence, emptiness after emptiness, nothing after nothing—in the darkness of the motel room her losses crowded around her like ghosts.

She would like to think of honeysuckle, of plucking its white blossom and finding inside it that little drop of sweetness. She would like to think of how nectar tasted on her tongue, and how the creek sounded, and how the bees buzzed, and how dark the woods were, and how unafraid she used to be. If only she could gather these details in her arms like wildflowers, cutting away the thorns and the poison vines, arranging them so that the whole was only pleasing, with nothing ugly winding up from the bottom to ruin the effect. If only, but she cannot. They cling to each other, these thoughts, one attached to the next, leading her back. They bloom overhead in hanging gardens, like the vines that crawl along power lines. They draw her along the roads they follow, the roads that lead always into the past.

The makeup artist gave Birdie Valium when she saw the dark circles under her eyes. *Try to sleep*, she had said, pressing the pills into her hand, so Birdie took one as she went to bed. There in the dark, as she waited for the pill to dissolve and enter her bloodstream, she listened to the sounds outside her door: the shifting of ice in the ice machine, the squeaky wheel on a passing cart, the hoses spraying down the concrete poolside, a key fumbling against a door's lock. She waited for that soft, empty feeling to arrive and when it did her thoughts poured out like water, out into the dark.

The crew liked to party and sometimes Birdie would join them. They celebrated the good days and obliterated the bad ones with whiskey shots and beer chasers, a twenty's worth of five-dollar specials for each of them, before staggering back out into the moonlit parking lot, their laughter falling silent as they listened to the buzz of cicadas and the calls of frogs rising up from the green-black trees. Once, toward the end, she let a camera assistant kiss her out there, pressed up against a production van, his mouth sweet from tobacco and Jameson. He had a silver earring that kept glinting in the moonlight and a few days' growth on his face. Gravel rolled and shifted beneath her feet. *Gentle*, she said as he kissed her, so that he would not leave her red. She asked him how she looked on camera. She wanted someone to tell her what she was. He wrapped his arms around her. *Small and pretty*, he said.

Then they did what they did. Two hours later he was saying how bad he felt, how guilty. He had a girlfriend he loved, he said. He rolled off her. He said he didn't understand how it had happened. She lay on her bed watching him dress, yellow-black shadows making everything terrible. She hated him already, his damp palms and his stumpy dick and how easily he bewildered himself. The clock radio kept blinking, reminding her of the nearness of their call times. How soon they would be out there again in the daylight, pretending not to know these things about each other.

When he was gone, Birdie opened the window. A moth as big as her palm hung on the screen. The drone of cicadas filled the room. It was the sound of something moving toward her, through the dark and across a great distance. She imagined their hard brown bodies approaching, their red eyes and stiff wings, their prehistoric bodies dragging through the trees.

Humid air pushed through the open window. On nights like this her mother used to say you could slice the air like bread. Then she would lie back on her bed, her palms pressed to her cheeks as if checking to see if she was still intact. Birdie would stand in the doorway and picture the air falling away in thick dark slices and piling up at her feet. She could eat the air if she had to, an abstract thought she had once found comforting.

The cicadas droned on. A light turned on in a room across the courtyard and the moth began to flutter against the screen. Great mouthfuls of air sat wet and sour in her throat. She went to the bathroom and vomited, but it was all still there, the air like bread in her mouth and the taste of whiskey and the taste of him. She needed to be rid of it.

She lay down on the bathroom floor and stared up at the ceiling. The fluorescent light buzzed above her. She punished herself with all of this, with the cold tile floor and with the dirt in the grout around the toilet and with the towels hanging just out of reach and with the moldy shower curtain touching her shoulder and with her rolling head and with her unmade bed, upside down through the open doorway. She stared up at that horrible light without blinking. She stared until everything buzzed and blurred and glowed white and her eyes filled with water and then suddenly a small truth descended like a fluorescent angel. That light Lewis saw wasn't heaven. It was his bathroom ceiling.

She laughed, a hard and dark sound that clattered over the tile like crickets. How horrible she was. She began to fill the bathtub. Deep inside the motel, water rushed through the pipes. The water rushed beneath her and above her and beside her, like blood in the veins of a great creaking body. When the tub was filled, she turned off the light and knelt on the floor beside it. She didn't want to see that light anymore. She dropped her face into the water, squeezing her eyes shut until she saw stars, and as the stars exploded and formed galaxies, she screamed and screamed and screamed.

55

"I said we had momentum," says Redmond, crossing his pool deck. Ice clatters into a glass. "I didn't say it was going to be easy."

"Easier," says Birdie, her towel over her face. She can hear him walking back toward her. She can feel the heat of the sun on her legs and stomach. She is uncertain how long she has been here; an hour or two maybe, but it feels like days. South Hill felt like a night, a dream. Time, that most basic of measures, continues to elude her. Her mother had once described God as having no beginning or end. *But when will He die?* Birdie had asked. Birdie thinks of Him now, vaguely eternal but still somehow older, hovering somewhere overhead.

How her mother had described the devil: if you saw him, he would be so incredibly beautiful. He would look like an angel of light and you would want to touch him and kiss him and lay your head on his shining shoulder. You would want to let him whisper in your ear. He would press his cheek to yours and pull you close to him. He would hold his palm against the small of your back. He would fill your ear with promises and ask you to say yes and you would say it just to hear how it sounded. Only then would you notice the stony bottom of his gaze and how the edges of the kitchen curtains lift in the breeze he brings with him, rising and falling as something leaves you, as he smiles against your neck and you grow cold in his arms, as he looks right past you.

Redmond places his hand on her shoulder and the cold

glass in her hand. Redmond, not quite beautiful enough to be the devil, otherwise she would have given him her soul a long time ago. He lifts the towel from her eyes. He is a shadow, an outline, and the sun shines behind him. "I never said that," he says.

56

She has been back for three days. With the exception of her single excursion to Redmond's, Birdie has remained home, occasionally venturing out onto the gray slab of her patio to sit in the sun, as she does now. For three days she has imagined the same scenario, which involves escape from Los Angeles and features Lewis as her costar. In her daydream they drive as aimlessly as they did in *That Day in Echo Park*, only they never stop. There is no taco stand, no 99-cent store, no return to Venice. Instead they keep driving until they leave the city behind them. They drive through California and Nevada and Arizona and Utah. They pass high cliffs that drop away into ocean and lush green forests lined with moss, great stretches of desert dressed with scrub oak and cactus, vast fields of oil wells pumping in unison, their towering black bodies sucking the dry earth drier. They drive until nightfall and then they drive a bit farther. They sleep in motel rooms and eat at diners. They drink at dive bars and shop at gas stations. They use assumed names. They pay in cash. They fuck in the shallow end of motel pools. They are fugitives from something nameless, uncertain of its progress. Sometimes they wake in the middle of the night and drive away, aware of its closeness. It is always three in the morning. Mountains are always in the distance. Their headlights always reveal rabbits darting through the dark, their eyes fluorescent green and wild. The truth, always known but never discussed, is that no one is actually looking for them. There is no chase. This is what they are running from:

the knowledge that they have disappeared and no one has noticed.

Lewis has called twice without leaving messages. Birdie should see him but she doesn't want to. When she sees him, the absurdity of her fantasy will be fully revealed to her. She will see how possible it is, how Lewis would actually do it if she asked him to. There would be no voice of reason. He would just hop in the car and drive her off into nowhere and then there they would be, in the middle of Bumfuck, sitting around looking at each other. How many times can you eat a cheeseburger and screw in a swimming pool? How many quarters can you put in the jukebox? And all the while, she'd be getting older. Her phone would be ringing. She could hear Redmond's voice already, sounding ever so slightly amused. *If you want to fail, my darling, fail locally. It's better for the environment.*

The neighbors are preparing for a party. Birdie watches from her patio as girls wearing black aprons and kitchen clogs shuttle large metal trays from a catering van to the kitchen. They arrange and organize and consult, their ponytails bobbing above achievable bodies. The producer's wife, barefoot and tan and wearing a silk kimono, stands in the garden with the gardener, indicating areas in need of attention. Then she disappears inside. The gardener stoops along the stone pathways arranging votives in glass jars along their edges while an assistant climbs trees, hanging paper lanterns from their limbs.

The phone is ringing. She lets it ring. She wants to stay outside on the patio and watch the gardener nudge each votive into place, dressing the landscape with calculated disarray. She does not want to go back inside, where empty glasses clutter the sink and her houseplants gasp and atrophy and dust bunnies sit in the corners of her rooms watching her with gray eyes. Inside, Lewis's breathing haunts her answering machine and the covers of her bed lump and rumple and the floor seems to shift beneath her feet. If only it really would. She doesn't mind earthquakes. After the walls stop swaying and the ground stops shifting and the shingles stop clacking, there is that moment when everything falls still. Sirens wail far away. Dogs bark. You taste dust in your mouth, pull plaster bits from your hair, and feel lucky to be alive. In that moment, she understands the appeal of apocalypse. How good it is to know the status of things, to know that you have survived.

The phone rings again and finally she walks inside and stares down at Lewis's number, familiar on the phone's screen. She answers before she can think better of it, just to make the ringing stop.

"Hi," he says. "You back?"

"Yeah. Just last night."

"Oh," he says. "I'm sorry. Did you get in late? Did I wake you?"

"No," she says. "I got used to the time change, so I've been waking up really early." She hasn't been waking early so much as not sleeping, but it is nearly the truth.

"Oh, right. Three hours ahead." A pause, and then the question she did not realize she had been avoiding until he asks it. "Well, tell me everything. How was it?"

Answering honestly would require a series of admissions that she was incapable of summoning: that she had a life she didn't want to remember, that *Where I'm From* was not the salvation she had mistaken it for, that whatever relief had filled her momentarily had drained away, leaving her empty again.

Never mind. He wanted to hear that it was all right. If everything was all right then his ambitions could remain intact, capable of rescuing him. So she would tell him it was all right. *Act as if*—isn't that what they always say—and you will transform into the person you pretend to be. If you can make other people want to be you, then eventually you will want to be yourself. You'll see their desire and you'll want, finally, what they wish for themselves: your own life.

She smiles. *Smiles, you can hear them.* She tells him it was wonderful. Then she asks him to come and see her.

57

Music plays through speakers hidden in the garden, an exuberant voice singing about summer. The gardener drives off in his little red truck, its taillights weak in the twilight. The sun is setting, but slowly, taking its time, hiding and seeking in the trees. Their limbs, once brown, are gray and silver against the sky and hung with glowing lanterns. Also in the trees: the silhouettes of birds. They turn their heads and twitter. They open and close their wings.

From her vantage point on her patio, Birdie can see the neighbors' guests arriving. They kiss each other and surrender their purses. They accept offered glasses and wander outside. Strelitzia plants sit in their beds, flowering orange and ready to be seen. Music echoes over the flagstones, a voice now singing about dreams, and just as this new song is beginning Birdie sees Lewis open her front door. The votives are flickering and Lewis glances around the living room and takes a step inside and the neighbors' guests lift their glasses and laugh and a cluster of startled birds darts up from the trees, a trio of black flashes against the sky, and in this way life is sometimes miraculous, as if it were all orchestrated for viewing pleasure, as if Leo King and Max Mason and Oscar and God were all sitting in an editing suite somewhere watching this very scene on a monitor. They say it together, like a Greek chorus: *You know what this needs? Music.* So as Lewis peers down the hallway, a song plays. A shaft of light hits his face as he walks into the kitchen and with illuminated eyes he says her name like a question: *Birdie?*

It is wonderful to see him looking for her. Pleasure is in being sought, not found. Did anyone ever say that? Birdie takes another sip of her drink. Someone should. Lewis is wearing his suit, of course, and a blue pin-striped shirt and an orange and white knit tie knotted at his neck. When he spies her through the open door he raises his hand as if he were hailing a cab, and though he is merely standing there in the empty doorway on the cusp of her little patio, it seems to Birdie that he is a point of stillness at a vast and treacherous intersection. The world is a background rushing past them, the sounds of laughter and the clinking of glasses and the colors of sky and the shadows of birds, and all Birdie wants to know is whether she will pass through the scene safely now that her costar has stepped through the doorway.

She stands to meet him and he wraps his arms around her and lifts her off the ground, burying his face in her hair. She lets herself go limp for a moment, dangling there in his arms. The weight of her body is terrifying. It embarrasses her how heavy she feels and she gasps a little and struggles against it, the conspiracy of scotch and gravity that drags her back toward the ground. Lewis lowers her gently and looks at her. "It's good to see you," he says.

She thinks very carefully about what to say next. She is keenly aware of the scene of escape still in her head, so vivid that she is afraid of speaking to Lewis for fear of revealing it. If she tells him, there is no return from the story's unfolding just as she imagined.

"Hi," she says finally. "Hi hi hi." She kisses his cheek and presses her palms against his lapels. She says, "Take off your jacket, Hank."

He told her how things had been. He quit his most recent temp job, the one at the penny stock company. He couldn't make it De Palma, no matter how hard he tried. There would be no final redemptive scene. He was no hero. He was just a person sitting in a rented office stamping the backs of Arizona checks and he didn't want to be an accomplice. That was the way it seemed to be these days. He didn't know what he wanted to be anymore, only what he didn't want to be. He didn't want to be a temp. It was so temporary.

Birdie sat there listening and nodding. She agreed with everything he said. He was right. This wasn't De Palma. He was right. Everything was hard and everything got corrupted. The world was terrible, she agreed. She tried to look into his eyes as she said these things, but she was looking past him, watching her scene of escape unfolding, the redwood forests and moss-covered rocks, the dusty asphalt and sun-plundered desert, the scrub oaks and jackrabbits, the red clay cliffs and unironic sunsets.

She told him none of this. Instead, she said she would speak to Redmond, to see if he could help find Lewis work as an extra. Lewis smiled and seemed both vaguely embarrassed and vaguely grateful. He was failing at everything these days, but he didn't want to be a failure. He had been working on a draft of *Seventeen Seconds* but the idea he had in his head was always much better than what he could get down on paper.

"Besides, even when I write something I like, I can never decide what comes next," he said. "Do you know what I mean?"

She nodded, looking past him at the empty frame of the doorway. She knew what came next. She saw a sad and beautiful scene in a motel room just off the highway, in some swampy Southern town choked with kudzu and churches. She is lying on the unmade bed and he is standing in the doorway. She has poured ice from the ice bucket into its plastic liner and is holding it against her bare stomach and she says *Well, what are we going to do?* and he says *I don't know.* He is staring out at the gravel parking lot and she watches a bead of sweat roll down his neck and she can hear someone yelling for their kid off in the distance, yelling *Get inside this very minute!* and she considers standing and walking across the room and putting her arms around him, only there is no comfort left in her. So he stands there not looking at her and she lies motionless on the bed. The ice melts into water. The television stares out at them, reflecting this scene on its darkened screen. She watches herself there, her body gray and convex, and in that moment she realizes what a terrible mistake it all was. A casting director once told her: *You're not right for television. Men may want to fool around with you but they sure as hell don't want you in their living room.* She closes her eyes and wishes herself elsewhere but there is no elsewhere. This is her life. And if she went anywhere with Lewis, they would wake one day with all of their scenes played, out of ideas and in need of an ending.

She was suddenly very aware of herself and the secret that she was now keeping, that there would be no Birdie and Lewis, or Birdie and Hank, or Birdie and whoever this was, whoever she had imagined him to be, her costar in this fantasy, and so she turned her attention to managing the position of her hands. These are the things that betray you, white knuckles when you should be smiling, arms folded across the chest in what should be a moment of candor. Reality is in the details, Otto always told her. So she held her glass in the center of her lap and relaxed her grip so that her knuckles maintained a nice normal color.

Lewis looked at her. "What is it?" he said.

"I'm just listening to you," she said. She smiled, she hoped not too broadly. She didn't know how to smile really, or more accurately, how to stop smiling once she had started. In order to stop, she had to do something else.

"No," he said. "You're thinking of something. What are you thinking?"

"I don't know," she said. "I guess I was reminiscing."

Lewis nodded slowly. "Yeah," he said.

"Remember that night at The Mount Maraca?" She allowed herself to look at him now, to look at his actual face. She looked not at his eyes but just below them, at the ridge of his cheekbone curving under his skin. He had freckles. "That was a good night."

Lewis nodded again. "Yeah," he said. He set his drink on the ground. "It was nice."

"The trouble with nights like that is that they're so wonderful, they make it harder for the other nights. It's not fair, to want every night to be like that."

Lewis looked at her. "Is that what you want?" he said. "For every night to be wonderful?"

"No, no. I mean, they couldn't all be wonderful. Or I guess they'd stop being wonderful. They'd end up just being your life."

Lewis nodded. He looked at her for a long moment without speaking. Her gaze fell away from his and focused on his cigarette's burning end, watching its path to his mouth and then back down again. Finally he spoke. "I know," he said. "I can tell."

"What? What can you tell?" She looked directly into his eyes and saw something terrible there.

"I don't want to talk about it," he said. "Let's just finish our drinks." He walked to the edge of the patio and stood there smoking and watching the neighbors' party. Birdie stared at his back, the movement of his shoulders beneath his jacket, the curl of his hair at the base of his neck. She was remembering him already, how he sat in a chair, how he smoked a cigarette, how everything he wore seemed borrowed. The party roared. There would be no final redemptive scene. That trip through the desert, the yellow light on the bed, the morning after the night before . . . none of it would happen.

She was crying. He walked over and crouched on the ground in front of her. He rested his palms on her knees and looked up at her. "What is it?" he said.

She shook her head. "Nothing."

He dropped his head and looked at the ground for what felt like a long time. "Hey," he said finally. "Just pretend it's a scene." He stood up slowly and spread his arms wide. "This is when he stands to say good-bye. This would be the moment to say something, if the girl has something to say."

She shook her head. He took a bow and walked away. Then she closed her eyes and the neighbors laughed and the music played.

58

"Let me give you three reasons to be happy," says Redmond. "Are three enough to get you out of this funk?"

A photo shoot is happening at Melena's next week, publicity for *Where I'm From*. Birdie and Melena will be photographed together, for *InStyle*'s "Sisters" issue.

Also, someone at Detonator Films told Redmond they want Birdie for *Light Year*. Well, not someone at Detonator exactly. A friend of a friend told him. Well, a friend of a friend of Carine's. She will have to audition but the audition will be with Rex himself. It is almost a sure thing, the audition. Time and location TBD.

Finally, Liz Orleans Casting has a call out for nonunion extras, for crowd scenes in a Nick Todd movie. Redmond promises to get Lewis in on it. A parting gift, he called it.

59

Melena answers the door herself, wearing jeans but naked from the waist up. She is smoking a cigarette and her hair hangs limply over her narrow shoulders. She air-kisses Birdie before waving her into the house and closing the heavy wooden door behind her. "I thought you were the stylist's assistant," she says, blowing smoke up toward the ceiling. "The dresses they brought are absolute shit."

"Oh," says Birdie. She stands in the entryway, unsure where to look.

Melena nods and turns to the dark wooden console by the door. On the console sits a large stone Buddha with crossed legs and closed eyes. She pulls a pack of cigarettes from his lap and lights another cigarette off the butt of her last one before stubbing it out on the ceramic tile floor. "Thank you, Jerry," she says, kissing the Buddha's head and stashing the cigarettes back in his lap. She pats his shoulder and glances up into the mirror hanging on the wall above the console. Smoke curls around her head and shoulders, lit by sunlight, giving her the appearance of a genie freshly sprung from its lamp. She grips the cigarette between her lips to free her hands and pushes at the skin above her breasts, pulling them upward, and then letting them bob back into position. Up, down. Up, down. "They're getting smaller," she says to her reflection. "The left one, especially. It's the fucking protein." She turns to look at Birdie. "Anyway, yeah. Loaners. They smelled like BO. They're coming back with more for me, but I think they were spraying something on the ones they brought for you. Like deodorant or something."

"Well, that's nice," says Birdie, trying not to stare at Melena's breasts. They regard her with curiosity, like another set of eyes. "Where are they?"

"One of the guest bedrooms." Melena waves her hand toward the hallway. "The crew is setting up by the pool. How original."

Birdie turns toward the hallway but Melena grabs her shoulder. "They'll get us when they're ready. Lesson one: they come to you." She waves her cigarette in a little circle to punctuate the thought, then walks down into the sunken living room and collapses on a large leather sofa. Birdie follows, sitting opposite Melena on a silk floor cushion. Through the sliding glass doors at the end of the hallway she can see a flurry of activity around the swimming pool. The *Evening Dawn* wrap party was only a few months ago. How long ago it seemed, her sitting on that pool deck with Redmond, still thinking that everything was solvable.

Beyond the living room in the open kitchen, an assistant is hunched over a large black platter, nudging slices of pineapple into concentric yellow circles. He glances up at them and then returns to his task. Melena turns to see what has Birdie's attention. "Trust me. He doesn't give a fuck about these." She stretches along the length of the sofa, arranging over her legs an orange cashmere throw embroidered with hundreds of tiny round mirrors. Crescents of light reflect up from the mirrors, scattering across the room like hundreds of little moons. They hang along Melena's tanned torso and nestle in the dark trench between her breasts "So. What a trip, right? Last time you were here you were still my ass."

"Oh, God." The mirrors send shots of light into Birdie's eyes, obscuring Melena from moment to moment. She buries her face in her hands.

"Hey, they showed me, like, twenty asses—LA asses, mind you—and I chose yours." Melena takes a long drag from her cigarette. "There are worse problems then having a good ass."

"I know, I know. It's just . . . I don't know. *Where I'm From.* This." Birdie gestures toward the activity on the pool deck. "I guess I still can't believe it."

"You can't? When I got *Mind Games* I was like, *this is it.* Sunshine Davis was just this evil sexy bitch. That part changed everything. I mean, I guess this isn't *Mind Games* for you, but you know. It's a step." She yawns and gestures toward Birdie with her cigarette. "Do you know what you're doing next?"

"Oh, I'm not sure yet. There's this Rex Peters thing potentially. But who knows."

Melena laughs. "Rex Peters! Oh, Gawwwd. Good. Luck. What is it? *Sex Planet? Crotch Rocket?*" She takes another long drag from her cigarette.

"*Light Year.*"

"Ha!" Smoke exits her mouth in a violent puff. "Let me guess. Sexy scientist?"

"Sexy alien."

Melena shakes her head and stretches like a cat. "God. You are so me five years ago."

Birdie briefly imagines stabbing Melena to death with one of the curved antique swords that hang on the wall behind the sofa. The scene she pictures is a sort of Japanese pop horror movie, vivid and symbolic, with the eye candy of red blood seeping into a snow-white carpet. But then the photo session would be canceled, so Birdie summons a laugh instead. "Well," she says. "That is kind of depressing."

"Come on. It's a compliment. Trust me, the beginning is the fun part." Melena leans on an elbow and stares down at her. Smoke leaks from her slack mouth, obscuring her eyes. "Seeing anybody?"

Birdie shakes her head. "Not really. I don't know. They come and go."

Melena laughs. "You ain't seen nothing yet." She leans forward and stubs out the cigarette. "Just you wait. Five years ago, you know, when someone wanted to fuck me, they wanted to fuck *me*, you know? Now . . . well you never know. You don't know who they're fucking or why they're fucking her. Most of the time, I figure it's Sunshine Davis because . . . you know. She was a total slut!" Melena smiles briefly at the thought. "Then they realize you're not Sunshine Davis. And they get all . . . *disappointed*. Talk about a head trip. Sometimes I'm just like . . . Fuck it. You want Sunshine Davis? You want some hot-short-wearing sociopath?" She lights another cigarette and leans forward. She is staring at something beyond the living room, some distant but real transgressor. She narrows her eyes and pokes him in the chest with her index finger. "Well, okay, buddy. You got it."

60

In the photograph, Melena stands on the top step of her swimming pool wearing a silver evening gown embroidered with heavy crystals that catch and split the light bouncing up from the water. Her hair is twisted into a golden coil at the base of her neck and she is looking directly at the camera, her famous smile half-formed, glossy white teeth gleaming between her barely parted lips. Clasped behind her back are her hands, hiding a lit cigarette. In the air above her head is a curl of smoke. "I love it," the photographer said. "You're so hot you're burning."

Birdie stands three steps below Melena, wearing a pink tulle party dress that floats like a jellyfish in the waist-deep water. Her limbs are coated with baby oil and sprayed with beads of water from a plant mister, giving her the appearance of having just emerged from the pool. Her hair, teased up into a froth of curls, hovers around her head like a cloud. "Like she is underwater and the hair is floating out," the stylist had insisted. And so too the makeup artist painted her eyes with blue and silver smudges, meant to be reflections from the water.

The entire scene seems held in place by the pillar of Melena's body, its gravity pinning Birdie to the water and the water to the swimming pool and the swimming pool to the veranda and the veranda to the hills and the hills to the sky stretched tight and blue above them. The photographer kept shouting, "Sexier! Not so sexy! Sadder! Okay, less sad!" and so Birdie kept adjusting her expression until she was tired from standing and cold from the swimming pool and when she glanced up at the sun to see how much time had passed, her face finally fell into something familiar. "Stay like that," the photographer said and so she did. She held herself still as she watched the sun slowly sink behind the veranda and the purple sky rise to take its place. Later, the photographer called her expression hopeful, but when he showed her the picture she saw a girl with a silly hairdo waiting for something to be over.

61

Birdie comes home to a message from Redmond saying the *Light Year* audition is a go. The script is on its way over and the meeting with Rex is the day after tomorrow.

That night Birdie dreams of a house by a river and a room full of trees. Outside, snow is falling. She lies on a bed beneath a dark green canopy of leaves. Lewis hides in the shadows, taking her picture from a distance. "Don't move," he keeps saying. It is suddenly very cold; she can see her breath. She rolls around the bed like the second hand of a clock. *Tick tick tick*. The camera's shutter winks in the dark.

In the dream, Melena is standing in the doorway. The cherry of her cigarette is a glowing point of heat in the gloom. She stares down at Birdie with her hair in her eyes. Then she turns and whispers to Lewis, who disappears into thin air when she says it, "Be sure to get her good side."

62

She was born on a planet a thousand light-years from anywhere. Only technically "she" is genderless. Technically she wasn't born. She is parentless but not an orphan. These beings spring from the ether. They emerge fully formed from the chemical stew of their planet's atmosphere. They are faceless and nameless and like humans in one way only. They are hungry.

So it is lucky that the American shuttle captain thought he heard a distress signal. It is lucky that the craft landed on the nameless planet that they decided to call Oberon. It is lucky that rescuing a person can make men feel powerful.

Picture three men in flight suits and round glass helmets slowly traversing the rocky surface of this planet. They see something suddenly, in the acid green light of their sulphur lanterns: a woman's limp body, naked and curled into a fetal position. Picture the look of terror in her eyes as they peer out at her, wall-eyed and mystified.

Technically it isn't terror. Technically it only looks like terror. The beings know how to be anything. They have assimilated every digital signal, every transmission, every airwave. They know every kind of human—and what each kind is best for—so she will be this beautiful, damaged woman that they pull from the shelter of a crater.

They call her Jane. Nobody knows how she got here. They wrap her in blankets and clean her wounds and let her sleep. Only technically they aren't wounds and technically she isn't sleeping.

Jane is lying on the sleeping platform blinking slowly, remembering that this is what they do. They blink. They smile. She looks at the unlocked door. She walks across the room and stands in the doorway. In the distance she hears the men talking and she moves toward the sound of their voices.

When she enters the galley they stand quickly in unison and insist that she sit. So she sits. They ask her what she remembers. She blinks. She says she remembers nothing.

She is alive. They look down at her proudly. They ask her if she is hungry.

She smiles. *Yes*. Technically, she is hungry.

On her way to the *Light Year* audition, Birdie sits at a stop-light on Gower and finds herself staring at a high cinder block wall scrawled with graffiti and crowned with loops of barbed wire. In the barbs are shreds of plastic bags, all different colors, lifted into the wire by the updrafts of passing traffic. A little breeze sends the shreds waving like flags, making them momentarily festive, then the breeze stops and they drop and hang limply along the wall.

Her focus shifts to her window and she sees a handprint there, too large to be her own. She wonders if it belongs to Lewis, the five long fingers held up like a traffic cop. *Stop.*

She should have told him how to do it, that being-an-extra business, how to walk straight ahead and shut out the rest. Just follow the sidewalk. Simple enough, but Lewis was always going in circles, looking back and then wondering what's next. What's next? No, not heaven. More sidewalk, Lewis.

Never mind. She looks past the handprint, back to the cinder block. She wonders briefly what is on the other side of the wall, what all of that barbed wire is protecting. What she thinks as she pulls forward: *Probably nothing.*

In real life, Rex Peters does not appear as he does in the photograph that hung on Byron Everett's *Wall of Fame*. His skin is still bronze and glowing, his pores are still invisible, his hair is still swept in a blue-black wave across his brick-shaped head, and his mouth is still full of perfectly square white teeth, but in person, the proportions of his face are faulty. One cheekbone is slightly higher than the other, as is one eye, and the cleft in his chin veers slightly off center, these factors combining to make the right side of his face noticeably better looking than his left. It occurs to Birdie that in Byron's photograph Rex had turned his good side to the camera, that he must always turn his good side to the camera.

As Birdie sits waiting for her audition, Rex describes to the director a mishap he had on a jet ski the previous week, what he calls a narrow escape. He windmills his arms around and lifts up onto one leg, illustrating his loss of balance. He dive-bombs his fist into his open palm and squats vigorously, illustrating the force with which he hit the water. He squeezes his eyes shut, pulls his hands to his stomach and releases a hearty, raucous laugh that seems out of place coming from his short, muscular frame. It is a fat man's laugh. The director, Grant Minger, laughs too, as does the casting director, as do the producers, Terry Hamlin and Lorraine King, both with Detonator Films. Rex claps his hands and grins. "Okay, okay, I'm sorry," he says. "No more stories." He takes a seat at the conference table and glances at the pages lined up before him on its surface. "What are we doing?" he says, gathering the papers without reading them into a thin stack. He fans himself with the pages and glances at Birdie. He says, "What am I supposed to be looking at?"

His ill-proportioned face peers up at her.

"I feel like I know you," he says. "Like I have known you all along."

"Maybe you have," she says, bending her knees slightly. "I feel it too." She rests her palms against his chest. She looks at his face, the veering cleft, the rogue cheekbone. She finds his eyes and closes hers.

Their mouths connect, his turning and opening, hers pliant and cooperative. His tongue, sour from nicotine gum, races along the ridge of her lower teeth as if he were counting them. Suddenly he puts his hands to her collarbone and pushes her away, to arm's length. "Wait a minute. Something's wrong," he says. He knits his eyebrows.

She steps back toward him. "Hold me," she says, grabbing his biceps. She runs her hands firmly along his arms and then she leans into him, pressing her breasts against his chest. "Closer," she whispers, her lips pressed against his neck.

He circles his arms around her waist and pulls her tight against his body. She feels his heart beating very slowly. He peers over her head at Grant and Terry and Lorraine. He says, "And then what?"

"You kill her," says Grant, from somewhere behind her head.

Rex looks down at her and smiles. He says, "I won't kill you for real, I promise."

65

"How did you do?" Redmond asked her.

"I'm too tall for him."

"Everybody is. The man is an extremely good-looking hobbit. Come on, you couldn't tell?"

"Redmond, you know I never can."

66

Waiting again.

At a friend of a friend's birthday party in Malibu, a music producer named Freddy backed her into a dark corner of the house's giant kitchen. The house belonged to him. Freddy was so rich that when he opened his mouth she expected a gold coin to come out, glistening with spit. Instead, he just said, "Hey there, dolly. Do your panties match your dress?" Her dress was purple, scattered with tiny black polka dots. Freddy grinned and slid his meaty fingers toward her, along the butcher-block counter. His wife, Chloe, was holding court outside on the slate veranda. Through the kitchen window, Birdie could hear her braying about her pregnancy. "Violently," she kept saying. "Violently, violently, violently!"

"What panties?" Birdie said, feeling reckless. She had been drinking chilled vodka out of little silver shot glasses that reminded her of thimbles.

A grub of a smile wriggled across Freddy's face. He pawed at the hem of her dress. "Lemme see," he growled, and pulled her toward him.

It felt good, occasionally, for something to actually happen. So she played along, thinking of Rex. *Oh, you stupid space captain. Don't you see what's coming?* She held her dress down with one hand and grabbed Freddy's tie in her fist. "Say please," she whispered, the way that Jane would whisper it, like an animal in heat. It wasn't hard to seem hungry. Rex would remember, wouldn't he, the feeling of her pressed against him and how her demeanor had changed like the flip of a switch. Judging by Freddy's expression, she was good at this, the more-than-he-bargained-for business.

Freddy pressed her back against the butcher block and got his face close to hers. Birdie looked past him, past the heat of his whiskey breath, at the bottles left empty on the counter, at the corkscrews, at the wooden block stuck full of knives. Sure. This could be some kind of space kitchen. Only there was the issue of Chloe's voice, floating up through the window. "Cesarean!" she cried.

"Look at me," Freddy said, and Birdie did. Rex was nowhere. Behind his dark glasses, Freddy's wet eyes were slowly blinking. He grabbed her wrist in his fist and licked his gray lips. He leaned close to her cheek and as he reached beneath her skirt he asked in a whisper, "Do you know what's good for you?"

67

On the drive home, the image Birdie keeps seeing is Chloe, rings flashing as she rubbed her swollen stomach like a good luck charm, her limbs bronze and slender, her smile serene. She came from nothing but got this far, as far as Freddy, on her beauty. She was a faux-tanned Mona Lisa from Alabama who used to be named Christine. Everybody knew but nobody cared, not anymore. Now Christine called herself Chloe. Now she had six figures' worth of diamonds stacked on her ring finger, weighed a hundred pounds soaking wet and six months pregnant, and occupied five hundred feet of Malibu coastline. However it might end with Freddy—and of course it would end, everybody knew that too—the golden egg in her belly was the only currency she would ever need. Birdie hated it already, the baby who would come squealing into this ridiculous family, Christine's eight-pound passport to being Chloe forever.

Back at home, Birdie slides into bed and lies still in the darkness with the phone cradled on the pillow beside her. She calls Redmond but he doesn't answer. He is at some other party, no doubt, laughing away at something that isn't funny. She leaves a message for him. "Whatever you hear from whoever's fucking tennis partner, just do me a favor and try to forget it. File it under vodka, okay? File it under desperate."

Then she plays her only message, Lewis saying that he had spoken with Liz, the extras casting agent, and she was giving him a few days of work on the Nick Todd movie, starting tomorrow. Crowd scenes. *Thank you so much*, he said, *I can't believe it*. He sounded like he meant it.

The ceiling hovers above her like the still quiet surface of a swimming pool. She is swimming along the bottom, her limbs heavy from the vodka. A black drain murmurs below everything, dragging her down through the water. She goes limp and floats into its dark interior.

She blinks and gasps. Her eyes are wet. She curls against her pillow and wedges the phone beneath her ear. She listens to Lewis's message over and over again so she can hear someone talking to her, someone saying that he is grateful.

68

She woke surprised to be alive. She had a dim recollection of a swimming pool and thought for a moment that she had drowned; then she remembered the party and wished that she had.

The phone lay on the bed, blinking. She had never heard it ring. There was a message from Redmond. "Got your message," he said. "Charming. The deal is: I'm not going to ask and you're not going to tell me." Then he said he had seen the pictures from the *InStyle* shoot. "They're good. You look *pretty*," he said. The word marched through her ear, tinny and small. She felt its ratatat in the hollows behind her eyes. *Pretty* never means *beautiful*.

Sunlight, acidic and white, shot through her bedroom window and scattered squares of light across the wall. Leaves rubbed against the window glass like little fingers, casting restless shadows that were soft at the corners and glowing inside. She lay in bed for a while, unblinking, watching the shadows and light advance along the wall and then up across the ceiling. She felt that she could lie there forever, the sunlight and shadow circling her in their gauzy orbits until she was wrapped tight as a mummy, bound to the bed by time, and if she only agreed to lie still, she would never have to leave.

69

Two weeks later Rex requested a callback and so Birdie went again to the low concrete building on Gower and waited again in the glass-walled lobby and shook again the producers' hands and listened again to Rex's story (an Appaloosa threw him when a burr stuck in the blanket beneath his saddle) and smiled again at everyone but no one in particular and stated again her name as they slated her and bent again her knees as she stood again in Rex's arms and pressed again against his body and said again her lines and kissed again his sour mouth and watched again as the expression on his crooked face changed and waited again for him to remember to pretend again to kill her and then walked again to her car and drove again home and lay again in bed trying again to fall asleep and stared again into the darkness and noticed again the loudness of her breath and as she tried again to fall asleep she hoped again that they would choose her.

70

There is news from Rex. "He likes you," Redmond says.

"How do you know?"

"Carine, of course. She takes Pilates with Sharon Metzner, who just happens to be Terry Hamlin's sister-in-law. Rex told Terry he thinks you're a firecracker."

"A firecracker?"

"That's good. With Rex, anything that explodes is good."

She sighs. "That's all? God, how long do we have to wait?"

Redmond's voice gets hard when he says, "As long as it takes."

71

How she knows the letter is from Lewis. First, it is a *letter*.
Second, he dots his *i*'s with stars. Two stars hover over her
name, scrawled above her address.

Birdie,

There are some things I think I should apologize for. If
I upset you, I'm sorry. It's hard to tell with you, whether
you're angry. You're a funny girl Birdie. You're hard to
figure out, but I liked trying.

I wanted to tell you, I tried to write *Seventeen Seconds*, but it didn't work out. I kept writing the same
scene. It's not a proper screenplay, but I need to show it
to you anyway. You'll understand I think. It's my movie,
so it's starring you and me. For once, I get to decide
these things.

Picture it. I am at my mother's house and you are with
me. You are in the kitchen making yourself a drink and
I am in my old bedroom, walking its perimeter, touching
the walls, remembering things. I sit on the edge of my
old bed and rest my hands on its ratty old quilt and listen as you shake ice in a cocktail shaker in the kitchen.
That noise, I don't know why it gets to me, but it does. It
sounds like something breaking. So I start wondering
why I feel this way, why I always feel like this. You keep
shaking the ice and I start thinking about how both of
us have lost things but you, you move on so easily. You

drink too much and you love too little but I forgive you for everything. I understand how life can be.

I sit on the edge of the bed and think of how you are strong and how I am weak. I think of how you made that call to Redmond and got me work as an extra, probably because you were feeling guilty, but also maybe because you love me a little. You just don't know it. Anyway, I never told you how it went. I wore a suit like they told me to, like I always do, and I showed up at the corner of 5th and Flower at five o'clock in the morning. On the drive over I confess I had a fantasy: I dreamt I would walk onto the set and the director would catch a glimpse of me and whisper in the producer's ear, and then they would approach me and give me a part, an actual part, and I would be so good, so real, so . . . everything. They'd be grateful to have me and amazed too that, before, I was only an extra. We'd all have a big laugh about it, at how wrong it was for me to be lost in the crowd. It's silly, but that's hope for you. It was a dream.

So I am sitting there on my old bed, in that room full of memories, thinking of what I wanted and then thinking of what was, of how I had walked back and forth on the same stretch of sidewalk twelve hours a day for three days straight. They kept yelling "Background!" and that was the signal to walk, because that was what we were. We were the background, moving out of focus behind the people that mattered, and we moved enough to make everything else seem real, like the actual world, but not so much that anyone would notice us. I was one of hundreds and I couldn't stand knowing that each of us was most likely wishing the same thing: that we would be the One. We all had the same lousy dream.

These girls on the sidewalk next to me kept flipping

their hair around and putting on lip gloss and asking each other how they looked and they kept saying to each other, You look good, You look great, You look beautiful, and you know, it was true. They were all beautiful but it didn't matter. Nobody was going to see them. What's the use of being beautiful if no one's going to see you? It was like being dead out there. I said so to one of those girls, I said I feel dead out here don't you? and she laughed and said that was a wish of hers, to play a dead body on a crime show. Picture it, she said, I'd play dead in a heartbeat, and then she stuck out her tongue and rolled her eyes back in her head. I did picture it. It was an image that appeared easily to me, all of us, shuffling back and forth in our best—the bright dresses and the pressed suits and the shining hair and the glossed lips and the ready hearts and the high hopes—all of us dead only we didn't know it yet. Everybody was still laughing and waiting and dreaming. They couldn't see, but I could. I could see that our whole lives are just a long death scene.

That day, that scene, has never ended for me. I sit in traffic on the freeway, I wait in line for a cup of coffee, I stand in an aisle of the grocery store staring up at the cereal boxes and I can see it so clearly now: this is just background. I walk through a parking lot, wanting somebody to notice. I've been hoping too much. I keep waiting to be chosen for something better, but nobody is going to choose me.

You stop shaking that shaker finally. I hear the sliding door and I know that you have poured your drink and taken it out onto the pool deck. It is a beautiful day, as beautiful as a day can be. I know you are sitting out there in a lounge chair with a blanket thrown over your legs, staring at the water. I don't want to meet you out there. I don't want to sit beside you anymore, wishing I could tell you something. There's no use in telling you anything. You always already know what I mean. I don't want to look out at that water and see what I always see, everything I have lost, floating there like dead leaves. So I stay in my old bedroom and stare at the wall in front of me. I feel what I feel.

This is the end of the scene. You hear a sound inside the house, an unmistakable sound, and you rise up out of your chair, screaming. I don't need to say this but you're beautiful even when you scream. You drop your glass and come running, the pool flat and blue and receding behind you. You know what it is, don't you, but you come anyway. You run towards the pain that waits for you behind the bedroom door and then you hold it in your arms, against your heart. You've never been afraid of pain, have you? I guess that's the difference between you and me. You would rock me to sleep, if I wasn't already sleeping. I know you would, because that would be the perfect ending.

Lewis

72

Lewis's phone rings and rings and rings. He won't answer, she knows. She lies down on the sofa and stares at the wall directly in front of her. She sees herself suddenly from outside her body. She feels the eye of a camera on her, measuring her grief on the screen. Everyone is watching. This is the moment where they want her to understand something. They need a tear to fall down her cheek and slide into her mouth, tasting of salt. More, they need more. They need to believe her. She squeezes her eyes shut and covers her face with her hands and takes a series of deep gasping breaths. Yes. This is what she looks like when she's lost something.

After a while, she walks to her bedroom and stands in the doorway, staring into the empty room. Headlights from the alley outside pass through the window, illuminating her body, her bed, her walls, before turning and leaving her in the dark. She saw a TV movie once where detectives went into a killer's basement, turned off the lights, and scanned the room with fluorescent wands. He had been so careful, but he had forgotten: you can never really get anything clean. The detectives stood in the darkness in their trench coats and stared, mouths agape, at the crimes mapped across the floor and the walls, glowing green in the dark like ribbons of stars.

She lies on the bed and turns off the light and stares down at the pale length of her body. This is what God is supposed to be: the eye that shines on your life and sees the harm that you have done. If he would only show her then she wouldn't have to wonder.

Only there are no eyes here. There are no patterns revealed. There is only the moon hanging in the window and Birdie lying alone in the darkness.

73

On one of their down days in South Hill, Birdie asked a production assistant to take her to a store where she could buy socks. What she actually needed was underwear, she had packed too few pairs, but she said socks because it was only her business what she needed. It was late and nothing was open except for one of those twenty-four-hour superstores that sells everything from frozen pizzas and scented candles to bedsheets and lawn mowers. The production assistant sat waiting in the van while Birdie went inside. As she crouched beside the display wall full of underwear, fumbling with the packets, trying to guess her size, she thought of Lewis. "Thank God I'm a Country Boy" of all things was playing over the loudspeaker and there had to be hundreds of different types of underwear, maybe thousands, and she imagined what Lewis would have to say about all of it and she kept hearing his voice in her head. *Candy and plastic*, that's what he'd call it, *a place full of stuff that just isn't broken yet*. Yes, yes, it was all depressing and monstrous and symptomatic of a larger cultural problem, a problem of homogeny and alienation, a need to consume both literally and metaphorically, a need to fill the holes inside ourselves, a need to disguise our greed by calling it need, but he wouldn't actually say these things. *What's the point?* That's all he would say. She didn't want to think about the point. She knew what came next in this line of reasoning: God and heaven again. She began to shake, her hands trembling as she sorted through the cellophane packets, because she was tired and because she could not discern her size on the graphic chart on the back of each label and because she was thinking of Lewis and now also the Apocalypse. She finally grabbed a package marked *Small* and stood in line and paid. She ran out into the parking lot away from that buzzing box of fluorescent light (birds were trapped inside and roosting along the ceiling), away from the lumpen people who heaved by her, all of these people she had narrowly missed becoming, their dull eyes tracking the linoleum and scanning their lists, their helpless children spinning beside them, those dirty little moons orbiting the silver grocery carts stacked with colors, filled with poison, rolling steadily forward. It was her own voice she heard describing this scene, insisting that they all were dying and that this was the world that was killing them. She did not believe in anything, but still she could imagine that all of this would end. Of course, Lewis would say that it will be all right. He would say that what matters is what happens next.

The production van sat like a waiting spaceship in a pool of light at the far end of the parking lot, and suddenly she was running toward it, her plastic bag dangling from her hand. She was afraid the van was going to lift off without her into the heavens. When she got back to her hotel room she opened the packet of underwear she bought and tried on one of the pairs but it didn't fit; the fabric puffed out around her hips like bloomers. She threw the whole packet into the trash and ignored the blinking message light and took one of the pills the makeup artist gave her and got into bed.

Lewis still thought he was going to solve something. He was twenty-one, young enough to resist, for a while, the things that would change him. Birdie was twenty-one too when she came to Los Angeles, running from something, and for that she had assumed she was courageous and special. Now she was thirty, almost everything and almost nothing. Lewis didn't know that she used to be like him. Everyone used to be like him. Everyone used to believe in something and then everyone changed. Lewis would change. Disappointment had set the clock ticking and adjustments would be made. Lewis would start cooperating, to be nice at first, because he thinks of himself as a nice person. He would laugh at jokes that aren't funny to be nice, have another drink to be nice, sleep with people he doesn't love to be nice, lie to be nice, and slowly Lewis would disappear. He would do things he never imagined. He would walk through the world unsure of what he was doing here, understanding nothing. He would buy his underwear in bulk, forgetting who he was.

That night in South Hill she lay on the bed in her motel room and out there in the dark, beyond her door, kids in the swimming pool were calling out to each other, "Marco." "Polo." "Marco." "Polo." They shrieked and laughed and splashed when they found each other, with the unabashed loudness of children. She was a child once. It seemed like a dream. Everything she had ever been seemed like a dream. She was a kid in a swimming pool, she was a kid in a dress preaching in the park, she was a girl in a movie theater, she was a girl on a bed, she was Judah's wife, she was a girl on a bus, she was Melena Duvall's body, she was a widow in Los Angeles.

Otto once said that over the course of your life you are actually hundreds of different people. You are a different person at the coffee shop than you are at the bar, and a different person for your dry cleaner than you are for your boyfriend, and a different person at work than you are on vacation. You are nobody in particular. But once somebody finds you and loves you, you have to keep being the person that they love. You want their love. You need to keep getting it, even if it means pretending. And so if they find you reading the newspaper in a coffee shop on Sunday morning, then that is who you must be forever. Somebody loves you. So you must wake up early and solve your crossword puzzles and drink your coffee.

But no one loved her and so she could keep changing. Lewis was gone, and so she was someone else already. It was better this way. If heaven actually existed and God actually existed and she ended up someday on that great white porch, which is how heaven usually appeared in her imagination, with a man who looked like George Burns, which is how God usually appeared in her imagination, they would look at the video monitor and review her life together, every last scene, and no matter what they saw, the truth of the matter would save her from judgment. No matter who she had ever seemed to be, she had changed. That girl—the one on the monitor—didn't exist anymore. She was history, whoever she was. Birdie was no longer that person.

74

Dear Beverly (Hills),

It's been too long. I hope that this is still your address, or that they will at least forward this letter to wherever you are. I'm sorry it took me so long to write back to you. I was glad to hear that you were doing well back home in Washougal and I guess I didn't want to reply until I had my own good news. You know how it goes here, though. Years can go by without any good news.

I'm in the same little rental in Venice, where I've been since I left our apartment. I'd been doing a lot of stand-in work, but I just finished shooting a part in a movie (with actual lines and everything) and I'm hoping it's a sign of things to come. Of course I'm knocking on wood as I write this.

I hope you are doing well and I would love to know what you are up to and how you are liking being back home. Have you met anybody special? I've had a few flings here and there but nothing special so far. I'm hoping something serious is right around the corner.

Oh, here is something that will make you laugh. Can you believe that Redmond is still my agent? He isn't with Joy anymore (big surprise) but he is really making things happen for me (finally). He is a patient man, clearly.

xoxo, Birdie

75

This time it's not the same. This time Rex Peters calls her himself to welcome her "aboard" this "odyssey." He looks forward to "piloting" this "ship."

This time clauses in her contract stipulate where, exactly, the various pieces of latex will be placed. Full rear, partial front. She walks out of the meeting with ink on her fingers, the geography of her body divided into territories, their boundaries defined and made legally binding.

76

On a legal pad, Birdie writes the following:

Jane (of Oberon).

Personal effects: None.

Family: None.

Food: N_{15}, a rare isotope of nitrogen. The human body is 3% nitrogen, hence her interest in it.

Sexual History: Technically asexual, but uses feigned sexual desire to advance her imperative.

Hopes: Hope is a concept unknown to her.

Fears: Fear is a concept unknown to her.

Hobbies: Survival.

77

These roads are familiar. It is dusk and the car carries her past all of the scenery she knows. Plastic banners and flags hang fluttering between the storefronts on Lincoln. At a stoplight, she watches three men, hammers in their hands, roost in a row along a rooftop like crows. They have stopped working and are watching the sun fall into the ocean. They are silhouettes.

She watches every person the car passes and thinks, *They don't know.* Her moment has finally arrived, only no one has noticed. The population of the world is otherwise occupied. They are rooting through shopping bags or murmuring into cell phones or licking ice cream cones or staring straight ahead through their windshields. They move forward when the light changes, taillights glowing red, their eyes on their destinations.

She is closer now, just a few blocks away. They inch along, the procession of cars stopping and starting and stopping again. She waits.

Beyond the rooftops and the trees, broad beams of light scrape the sky. Like a manhunt in reverse the spotlights search the heavens, anxious to confirm that there is nothing up there, nothing that might threaten what lies supplicant beneath these endless red carpets: the spangled, lovely earth. No, the heavens contain only smog and stars and those stars are more distant and less glittering than these, rising up out of the limousines, teeth shining, eyes sparkling, too beautiful to be believed.

It's time, Redmond says.

He releases her hand. The door opens and the crowd is shouting and this is the photograph that will join the others on Byron Everett's Wall of Fame—he will remember, of course, and lay claim to her—Birdie Baker smiling, beautiful, wearing a gold dress that fractures the light from the flashbulbs into millions of little pieces. A girl will sit in his chair and look up at the picture and when Byron asks her what she wants she'll say *That*.

What, he will say, sighing.

Then she will say, *I don't know exactly*.

The crowd is screaming. A voice on a loudspeaker shouts her name to them. A spotlight finds her body and holds her steady in its wide pool of light. She glances back at Redmond, who stands, like a cast shadow, three steps behind her. He gestures for her to turn and face the crowd and so she does. She takes a step forward. *Be like ginger ale*, she thinks, *effervescent and golden, sparkling and sweet. Make them want to drink you*. She smiles and the wall of bodies strains against the police line. She feels the mouth close around her. She waves. Cameras flash and there is the white noise of screams. She feels herself being swallowed. Everything is bright. She is looking past all of them, past everything, into the sea of white light.

78

Ask Birdie how she got here and there will be no recitation of losses or wistful recollections. In lieu of detail she may mention how ordinary it all was. *Pretty forgettable*, that's what she'll say. She'll laugh and glance down into her glass. *Honestly*. She'll watch the ice cubes melt away.

Sometimes there is a drive home from a party, Redmond at the wheel beside her, and she will find herself on the brink of sleep. Her head will roll forward and in that instant, if the windows are open and the night is fragrant with trees, she will disappear into a dream that always seems to be waiting for her to reenter it. The dream is of her grandmother's house. Here is the painted wallpaper, the solarium full of orchids, and the great magnolia dark and heavy with leaves. Here is the courtyard full of statues, salt-white in the moonlight. Here is the smell of honeysuckle and the buzz of crickets and the bubbling fountain, its stones slick with moss. Here is her penny, lying hard and shining at the bottom. What did she wish for? She doesn't quite remember.

Sometimes Redmond stops abruptly and Birdie opens her eyes and remembers suddenly that she had wished for another life. She looks over at him and his face is bathed in red light. He seems beautiful. It is possible that he loves her. He smiles. She hears sirens in the distance and on the breeze she smells the smoke from wildfires. Somewhere a city is burning. He presses his hand to the steering wheel and she notices the pale white crescents at the base of his fingernails and the glint of his watch inside his jacket sleeve, and for a moment she feels grateful.

We're almost there, he always tells her, but she never quite believes him. So she turns back to her open window. She closes her eyes and lets the dream reclaim her.

Here is the darkness of that summer garden. The wish is wished. Everyone is sleeping. The statues stand frozen in the courtyard, ivy wound around their broken necks. They regard the girl with empty eyes. Inside the glass walls of the solarium, the orchids bow and sigh.

79

She doesn't remember it being a decision exactly, only that the yellow truck arrived and two men carried the contents of her bungalow out in thirty-four cardboard boxes, two by two by two. Thirty-four seemed like too many and also too few, but that's how everything felt, like too little and also too much. The boxes were small and lightly packed and numbered, their contents inventoried on a sheet of paper and then loaded onto the truck and deposited in a storage space in Culver City. The inventory list read like this: mirror, votive holder, cocktail shaker. Birdie felt for a moment like an archaeologist reviewing the remains of an ancient village. The team would want to know: Who lived here? What became of them? How did they live? Who were their gods? Sift through the dust and tell us.

The producer's wife wandered barefoot across the lawn to collect the keys—Claire was her name, how could Birdie have not known her name this whole time?—and remarked on what a good tenant she had been. So quiet, Claire said. Almost invisible.

At Redmond's, Birdie arrived to a room filled with flowers and a white duvet arranged just so on top of their bed. She stood in the doorway for a moment staring at the bed, afraid of its perfection. Her mind slid over the idea of making adjustments, of fixing things, but there was no need. Redmond had taken care of it.

Birdie watches him now through the sliding glass doors. He is on the pool deck stretched out in a lounge chair, speaking into the earpiece of his phone. Smoke rises in the hills behind him. He is shirtless and tan, his sunglasses staring skyward, gesturing with his hands. She guesses now what he is saying: that it is not enough. His head is shaking and his hands fly upward—no, it will never be enough—but he will invoke a higher power. He will talk to the boss and to the boss's boss. He will strike a bargain.

All of this is different from what she expected, though in what way she cannot say. She does not know what she expected exactly, only that she wanted to feel changed. Sometimes it seemed that the only thing that had changed was the furniture. The house was decorated with armless chairs and one-armed chaises and a few small, menacing ottomans. Once, toward sunset, in the house's darkening rooms she saw the ottomans out of the corner of her eye and mistook their little figures for those of crouching children. She stood perfectly still, afraid to move, until she told herself what they were. They were nothing that could hurt her. When she told Redmond what happened, how ridiculous it was that she was afraid of the ottomans, he snorted and laughed and said, *What did they ever do to you?* But in the morning, the ottomans were gone.

Sometimes she sees her life as a series of set pieces rolling in and then out again, realistic enough to fool the camera but unable to withstand closer examination. Any inspection would reveal the flatness of everything, the false walls and painted-on doorknobs, the paper and paste in which everything is rendered. She would like to see it as the camera would see it. And so she keeps her distance.

She places a hand on the cool glass of the sliding door, conscious suddenly of her reflection there, the transparent likeness hanging in front of her, but she looks past it, she can't go to that place, the place her reflection takes her. She has a dim memory of a girl wearing peach silk underwear trimmed with bits of yellow tulle lying across an enormous bed and for a moment she thinks it is herself that she is remembering. Then she looks down at her hand, the fact of her hand, its blue veins visible beneath her skin, and becomes real again.

She finishes her drink and goes to lie down in the bed and shuts her eyes and waits to hear the sound of the glass door sliding open and then closing again, the footsteps advancing in the hallway and then, those words whispered softly— *Another victory, my darling*—and she turns and kisses him, sleepy and thankful. Then she sleeps under covers as deep and white as snowdrifts.

The role is a good one. The woman is beautiful but ignorant, ambitious but fearful. She hides. She assumes false identities. She lies. She is rejected, debased, adored. Sometimes she wakes up screaming. These scenes take place in fields and cities, hotels and rented houses, by the bluest of oceans and on the low banks of rivers.

What Birdie likes best is the ending. The woman faces her fears, makes amends, forgives and is forgiven. She is free, finally. In the final scene you see her driving a convertible, oceanside and with the sunrise behind her. Her hair is flying out around her shoulders and she is playing the radio loudly, singing along to some silly song. The road ahead of her stretches out into infinity.

Redmond thought the end was too easy, but Birdie said that was the point. *It's a movie*, she told him. *Let it be easy.* Nothing else is. This is how everything should end: with the forgotten remembered, the wounded healed, and the sinners forgiven.

acknowledgments

A thousand thanks to my early, enthusiastic readers: Taylor Antrim, Callie Wright, Laura Dave, and Colin Mort. For generous support when it was most needed, thanks to the Vermont Studio Center, the Sewanee Writers' Conference and the Ledig House International Writers Residency. Thanks are also due to my brilliant teachers at the University of Virginia and to Linda and Susan at Glimmer Train Press.

I am indebted to Bill Clegg for his guidance, enthusiasm, and unwavering support. And I am so grateful to my wise and wonderful editors, Marjorie Braman and Lindsay Ross.

Finally, for all manner of faith and friendship, my heartfelt thanks to: Diane Arute, Mary Arute, Jaime Boulter, Jennifer Brooks, Katy Caldwell, Joe Cohen, Amy Crilly, Kate Davis, Tess Dixon, Eileen Hollowell and Lonnie Hicks, John Hollowell, Bronwen Hruska, Bob Kaputof, Sherri Levy, Ryan and Melissa McNeely, Alex P., Kim Sharp, Wendi Weger, Roy and Alyssa Wilhelm, Kathleen Winter, my parents, my darling Lowe, the inimitable Serge, and my one true Daron.

etc.

extras…

essays…

etcetera

more author
About Jenny Hollowell

more book
About *Everything Lovely, Effortless, Safe*

…and more

Meet Jenny Hollowell

Amy Crilly

Jenny Hollowell's short fiction has appeared in *Glimmer Train*, *Scheherezade*, and the anthology *New Sudden Fiction*, and one of her pieces was named a distinguished story by Best American Short Stories. She received an MFA from the University of Virginia, where she was a Henry Hoyns Fellow in Fiction and recipient of the Balch Short Story Award. She lives in Los Angeles with her husband and daughter. This is her first novel. ◼

Birdie leaves home because she cannot embrace her family's religious evangelism, yet the fame she hopes for requires nearly the same leap of faith as the next life her parents are awaiting. What is the connection between Birdie's and her family's respective desires to be transformed?

Everyone wants to feel their life is important in some way. Whether you are in church on Sunday or in line at an audition for a reality TV show, I think you are revealing a very basic human desire. You want to be seen by someone, really *seen*. You want to know that you matter. I don't think it is a coincidence that our culture is so captivated by fame and religion at the same moment. To me, these obsessions are not contradictory. They are illustrative of our desire as human beings to feel our lives are meaningful.

Both pursuits require sacrifices. Birdie's parents spend their lives devoted to their evangelism. They don't have hobbies or social lives or anything that might be perceived as self-centered. There is no doubt they have selfish desires—they are human, after all—but they have subjugated them to keep God at the forefront of their lives.

Having lived in a household that ran on faith, Birdie naturally has these same resources. She is very much her mother's daughter in the sense that she has staked everything on one hope. The sacrifices Birdie makes—delaying gratification, enduring ridicule, accepting uncomfortable circumstances in the pursuit of a greater reward—are behaviors she learned from her family. In a way, faith is the family business.

Was your own religious background on your mind as you were writing this novel? How did it affect your thinking about Birdie's relationship to faith?

I grew up in Virginia in a very religious family. We were Jehovah's Witnesses, a Christian religion, though I think most mainstream Christians see it as pretty radical because of the Witnesses' door-to-door evangelizing work. I am no longer an active member of this religion, but my parents are. Though these circumstances result in conflict from time to time, we manage to have a very positive relationship. Our family dynamic is very different from Birdie's, thank goodness.

Although my background clearly informs many of the religious references in the book, I avoided naming any specific religion for a few reasons. First, the book is not a critique of a particular religion or its believers. I am no longer a religious person, but I understand the desire to have faith in a specific outcome—a sense of destiny, if you will. I am not prosecuting that inclination. Rather, one of my intentions with the book was to focus on the commonalities between those who express their faith through religion and those who express it through other ambitions. Though Birdie's goals are not expressly spiritual, they require great faith regardless.

Second, the conflict between Birdie and her family isn't really a theological one. Yes, there is the matter of Birdie's abandoning the religion of her childhood, but her conflict, stated generally, is relatable to anyone: how to navigate the disparity between your parents' expectations of you and the life you imagine for yourself. Your parents may not want you to evangelize . . . but perhaps they have mentioned you really should go to law school? *Art*, they keep telling you, is simply not practical.

I had a baby daughter as I was finishing the book, an experience that made me think further about the nature of the conflict between Birdie and her parents. I found myself sympathizing with her parents more than I had before. Though their choices seem pretty radical, they simply want what every loving parent wants: a long and happy life for their child. Of course, especially now, I relate to that desire very much.

How did Birdie's encounter with Wes change her or shape her future?

Until she met Wes, Birdie had only practiced being someone else at home in her bedroom mirror. That preening and posing was clearly just a dress rehearsal. With Wes, she takes her act out into the world.

It is an encounter driven by desire, but not of the sexual variety. Yes, Birdie loses her virginity, but what she desires, I think, is to do something irrevocable. Sex is irrevocable, so the encounter is a way for her to permanently change who she is. She is tired of just posing in front of the mirror. Think of the old question: If a tree falls in the forest and no one is there to hear it, does it make a sound? Alone in her bedroom, Birdie lacks impact. But with Wes, she has an audience. She makes a sound.

What she discovers is her ability to be convincing. She can make a person (in this case, Wes) react to her the way she wants them to. She can elicit desire. She can shut down parts of herself—deaden her emotions, really—in the interest of playing a character. This experience sets a precedent for the ways in which she will use sex in her adult life. Her relationships with men have little to do with love and everything to do with playing a part and testing her power.

Birdie feels terrible guilt about Judah's death, far more than she seems to have felt about abandoning their marriage. What makes her react so strongly?

More than anything, I think Birdie is feeling survivor guilt. Had she stayed with Judah, had she been the devoted wife that she should have been according to her religious upbringing, she would have been in bed beside him on that night and would also likely have died. She survived because she left. There is a terrible irony in being spared death as a result of breaking her vows and abandoning her marriage.

Judah's death also increases the pressure for Birdie to succeed. Birdie, like her mother, has staked everything on a happy ending, that "final redemptive scene." She is no longer a student of the Bible, but she cannot stop seeing the world in terms of condemnation and forgiveness. If she can *make it*, her life up to that point—including Judah's death—takes on a kind of biblical logic. It was painful, yes, but an inevitable part of her journey to the reward. *Making it*, therefore, becomes equivalent in her mind to forgiveness for any pain she has caused along the way.

Lewis enters Birdie's life at a crucial moment, when she's teetering on the brink of success. What does Lewis represent to Birdie, and what does she need from him?

Initially, Birdie simply enjoys the attention she gets from Lewis. She is at a moment of career crisis, feeling depressed about the prospect of doubling for Melena on yet another movie, and Lewis comes along—this terribly good-looking, albeit oddly dressed, young actor—and tells her how impressed he is by her. What she views as evidence of her failure—the fabric softener commercial in particular—he sees as a major success. He is just the medicine her ailing ego needs. Of course, when Lewis begins unpacking his personal baggage Birdie quickly loses interest. The whole point of that initial night together was to escape reality and to be simply worshiped. She didn't want to be the sounding board for some emotionally unstable kid.

But in the aftermath of Jules Dylan's party, Birdie decides she needs Lewis. Specifically, she needs his *realness*. Max told her she was *real* (as Leo had). But the party leaves her feeling like just another Hollywood phony. She realizes the very quality that made her memorable to Max is in jeopardy. Earnest, naïve Lewis, wearer of vintage suits and author of handwritten notes, seems to offer an affirmation of her *realness*. So she calls him, eager to retain what she fears she is losing. If you want to get reductive, calling Lewis after that party was essentially a career decision.

Was there a particular person or story that inspired Birdie's character? Where do you look for inspiration when you write?

I have freelanced in television advertising for a long time, and part of the process of making a commercial is casting actors. I cannot begin to count the number of casting tapes I have watched over the years and the number of callbacks I have attended. For any given role you might have a hundred people auditioning and you know that only one of them can get the part. The odds are so daunting to get even a television commercial, much less a role in a film. It is pretty depressing if you start to think about the odds . . . and I guess I did. I started wondering what that life must be like—the constant rejection, the pressure to "make nice" with the very people rejecting you, and the matter of what to do with your feelings about all of it as you walk in to your next audition. There are so many factors at work: age, appearance, talent, connections, charisma, and plain old luck. I thought it must be very hard to know what one can do to be successful in that business.

The story of how Birdie came to be a character

provides some insight into where I find inspiration more generally. I like to write about anything I do not understand. As you can imagine, this gives me loads of material. In this case, the ambition to be an actor just completely stumped me. I could not fathom why anyone would choose such a difficult path.

How have you been influenced by the culture of Hollywood, and of Los Angeles in general?

As I mentioned, I have worked in advertising for years, and long before I lived in Los Angeles I worked there, staying in hotels for long stretches of time while I produced various TV commercials. Because I was staying in certain hotels and eating at certain restaurants, I would see movie stars with surprising frequency. Sometimes I wouldn't even realize they were famous at first—I would think that I knew them because they looked so familiar. It is a little surreal to recognize someone when they clearly don't recognize you. There is an inequality to that relationship that is completely inescapable for everyone involved. You can think you are the sort of person who doesn't care about that kind of thing, but when you are sitting in a hotel lobby with Harrison Ford it is kind of hard not to notice him.

If you spend any significant time working in production in Los Angeles, you have these experiences. You meet famous people, you work with them, and their levels of wealth and success can be shocking. For anyone trying to "make it" in Hollywood I think that proximity would be profoundly frustrating. You are *this close*, literally, to the people who have what you covet. I thought about this proximity a lot when writing the book. ▪

Birdie's story originated with a small scene I wrote back in the spring of 2003. I was living in Charlottesville, Virginia, and approaching the end of my MFA program. I had an idea for a story about an actress who lost the ability to tell when she was acting, but it never quite came together. I wrote one scene with an actress character named Birdie but I quickly felt that the scope of what I wanted to say went beyond the confines of a short story. I didn't feel ready to work the idea into something longer and so I set the scene aside.

I moved to Brooklyn the summer after finishing graduate school and for the next year and a half I wrote pretty rarely. I told myself I wasn't writing because New York was so expensive and I needed to work, but I think I was also a little burned out from my MFA program and needed some time to recharge and think about what I wanted to write next. On some level I knew that I wanted to write a novel, but I was in denial about that.

Finally, in December 2004, three friends from my graduate program who were also living in New York proposed doing an informal workshop together. Our first meeting was to be on February 9, 2005. I didn't have anything to show them yet, but I said yes just to give them the impression that I was being productive. In truth, I had successfully avoided writing for nearly eighteen months.

As of late January I had written nothing. I looked back at the Birdie story from UVA in the hopes of polishing it into some kind of respectability, but it was just terrible. There was nothing I wanted to retain except the idea of a story about an actress named Birdie. I was just

9

coming to terms with the fact that I would actually have to write something new when I got terribly sick with the flu. Rather than derailing me, my sickness and that impending workshop deadline created a perfect storm of motivation in me. I was between freelance jobs—in plain terms, unemployed—and I was living alone in this tiny apartment and after two days of watching cooking shows and *Law & Order: Criminal Intent*, I was bored beyond belief. So in this kind of pathetic, fevered state I decided to sit down and write for a little while and see what might happen. So I did. In fact, I inflated an aerobed on the floor of my study so I could write lying down. In retrospect, I don't know why it didn't occur to me just to go write in my own bed, but it had some kind of logic at the time. I think I was feeling sorry for myself and was hoping to channel Proust or something.

Anyway, I write on the computer and save my drafts pretty obsessively, so I can look back and see that it was on January 23, 2005, at 10:18 a.m. that I wrote the very first page of what would eventually become this book. Over the course of the next week I wrote about fifteen pages. At our first meeting, I shared those pages with my workshop group. I was superstitious about calling it a novel because I was sure I had no idea how to write a novel, so I called it "the project." The workshop went well. My fellow writers told me what you should always tell someone who has just started working on a novel, which is just *keep writing*. It was wonderful advice and I completely ignored it. Over the next eight months I took a string of demanding freelance jobs and also got married. I wrote only twenty more pages, just enough to get me through my next workshop meeting. As 2005 drew to a close I realized that I had finished exactly thirty-five pages in nearly a year and I either needed to commit myself to "the project" or simply abandon it.

So I attacked the book with renewed zeal and by October 2006 I had finished a draft. It wasn't very good.

Most of the characters that would ultimately populate the novel were there, but the story was a mess. Lewis was a minor character and the acting teachers had a bunch of long speeches about truth and commitment—real yawners. The emotional weight was in all the wrong places. When I reread the draft and acknowledged how much work it needed, I applied for a fellowship to the Vermont Studio Center. I felt that the only way I was going to finish a revision was to focus on it exclusively, with no distractions.

Thankfully, VSC offered me the fellowship, and in February 2007 I went for a month. While I was there, Vermont had record cold and snowfall. Some mornings I had to make my way through waist-deep snow to get to my writing studio. Trudging through that snow was an apt metaphor for the process of revision. I was slowly making progress, but it was a cold, uncomfortable slog.

I made another monthlong trip to VSC a year later, in January 2008, and then finally finished the revision in May. My husband and I left New York and—with me now pregnant—arrived in LA later that same month. Some of my friends have joked that I wrote the book and then proceeded to *move into it*, as we ended up living in a little bungalow in Los Angeles just two weeks after the book was finished. I never really thought about it that way, but perhaps there are therapists who would be interested in helping me consider the implications. I worked on a few edits over the course of that summer, and I must admit it was weird to suddenly be living in the city where the novel was set. Everywhere I went there were reminders of the world I had inhabited, mentally, for the four previous years. Suddenly it was all physically manifest.

One incident in particular made an impression on me. I was sitting in a coffee shop one day, making a few tweaks to the manuscript, and the bell on the front door rang as someone walked in. I looked up and standing there was this very beautiful but unsophisticated-seeming young lady. It was Birdie. This woman was exactly who I pictured Birdie to be when she stepped off that bus from Virginia. Her shoes were wrong for her bag and her hair was wrong for how beautiful she was. She glanced over at me—I was staring at her with my mouth hanging open—and gave me a dirty look. It was exactly the kind of look Birdie would give a person like me, some random disheveled pregnant lady staring at her in a coffee shop. It was perfect. Then she grabbed her coffee and turned around and walked away. This particular coffee shop has lots of regulars, including myself, so I keep expecting to bump into her again. But I haven't seen her since. ■

This book was written over the course of several years in many different places—New York, California, Vermont, Arizona, Tennessee, and Virginia—so I was very much in need of some sense of continuity. I would often find myself at a desk in an unfamiliar place, staring at a scene I had written two years earlier, and I would need a way to reconnect with it. Music provided that for me. No matter where I was, or *when* I was, I could listen to a certain song and it would take me back to the feeling of a particular scene. These songs became a kind of soundtrack for my writing process.

When I think about my favorite films—*The Graduate*, for example—the songs in its soundtrack become forever linked to the movie for me. When I hear "The Sound of Silence" I always picture Benjamin and Elaine riding away in the back of that bus. They are inextricably connected in my memory. In a similar way, when I hear the following songs, I will forever remember the writing of this book.

1. "Pyramid Song"–Radiohead

According to my iTunes player, I have listened to this song 843 times. A bit of math reveals that means I have spent 67 hours, 40 minutes, and 45 seconds of my life listening to this song, most of that time as I wrote. I suppose I love it. Of course, the problem with loving Radiohead is how unsurprising it is. It is like loving Van Gogh. Everyone agrees the guy knew how to paint a picture. So I acknowledge I am not exactly going out on a limb here. That said, this song really is wonderful. It opens with a few dark, quiet piano chords that ever so gently begin to propel you forward. Then the percussion comes in, jazzy and full of swing but slightly off-time, which creates this funny kind of lag. Orchestral strings swoop in, along with Thom Yorke's howl, creating these little lifts before dropping you back down into that murky piano progression. The result? Every time I hear this song I feel like I'm being dragged across the bottom of a lake. I mean this in the best possible way.

2. "Ice Water"–Cat Power

Maybe it's the Southern thing, but Cat Power always gets me in the mood to write about Virginia. Despite its title, this song is actually *humid*. I heard it played in a Brooklyn bar once and it seemed a most bizarre breach of context. This song should never be played anyplace that doesn't have a porch. I get mosquito bites just from listening to it.

3. "In the Morning"–Junior Boys

At one point I was working on the book while dog-sitting in Tucson, Arizona, and the dog would wake up at five o'clock every morning wanting to be let out. He was very old and very adorable so what could I do? I would get up, let the dog out, make some coffee, and sit down at the computer to write. The problem was, it was 5:00 a.m. and the chapter I was working on was a party scene. How do you write a party scene at five o'clock in the morning? By listening to a song like this.

4. "All the World Is Green"–Tom Waits

I confess I have never written a word *while* listening to Tom Waits—I am usually too busy working on a glass of wine—but his music always puts me into a creative frame of mind. I love this song's tipsy, carnival quality. It manages to be celebratory and sad at the same time. I find myself swaying to it long after it stops playing . . . or maybe that's just the wine.

5. "Wolf Like Me"–TV on the Radio

I spent two months working on this book in Vermont during the dead of winter. There was three feet of snow on the ground and I was spending eight hours a day in my writing studio, sometimes actually writing. But if I found myself just staring at my computer screen—which happened more often than I would like to admit—I would trudge up the hill to the local college gym to run on their treadmill. I hate running, but when I am feeling uninspired I find that running knocks my brain around a little bit and gets the thoughts moving again. This song was my treadmill soundtrack of choice, though it is certainly not your average cardio fare. Yes, it is incredibly propulsive, but also so dark, with these menacing, sexy lyrics that mention *werewolves* and *day rates* in the same breath. Werewolves, day rates . . . of course it made me think of Los Angeles.

6. "I Wanna Be Adored"–The Stone Roses

This song was the cornerstone of my adolescent angst. For at least two solid years, every tear I shed while pining over some unrequited crush was initiated by the act of putting this cassette tape into my pink boom box and pressing Play. Sigh. So when I needed to put myself into the mind of a teenaged Birdie, I listened to this song.

Did I mention the poster of James Dean hanging over my bed? Or the poster of Morrissey in a Euro-cut bathing suit, lying next to a pool and reading *The Herald-Tribune*? Good God. It's true, all of it.

7. "Glósóli"–Sigur Rós

I read an interview with Chuck Palahniuk where he said he uses music like a drug, to induce a certain state in himself when he writes. When I considered what music has a similar effect on me, I immediately thought of Sigur Rós. This song seems almost subliminal to me—listened to on headphones, it puts me into a kind of trance. When I am writing, this is that rare song I can listen to without ever actually *hearing* it.

8. "Don't Think Twice, It's All Right"—Bob Dylan

I listened to this song a lot as I was writing the end of the book. Bob Dylan always gets me in the mood for a conclusion. He is so good at summing things up, distilling a world of complications into a few pithy lyrics. I love the harmonica in this one too. As an instrument, the harmonica seems uniquely able to communicate sadness and happiness simultaneously. I suppose it is the sonic equivalent of my favorite kind of ending. ■